SHADOW OF A BULL

SHADOW OF A BULL

Maia Wojciechowska

Aladdin Books
Macmillan Publishing Company
New York

Aladdin Books
Macmillan Publishing Company
866 Third Avenue, New York, NY 10022
Collier Macmillan Canada, Inc.

Second Aladdin Books edition 1987

Printed in the United States of America

A hardcover edition of *Shadow of a Bull* is available from
Atheneum Publishers, Macmillan Publishing Company.

10 9 8 7 6 5 4 3

Library of Congress Cataloging-in-Publication Data

Wojciechowska, Maia, date.
  Shadow of a bull.

  Summary: Manolo Olivar has to make a decision: to follow in
his famous father's shadow and become a bullfighter, or to follow
his heart and become a doctor.
  [1. Bullfights—Fiction. 2. Spain—Fiction] I. Title.
PZ7.W8182Sh   1987   [Fic]   86-22199
ISBN 0-689-71132-8 (pbk.)

SHADOW
OF A
BULL

1

When Manolo was nine he became aware of three important facts in his life. First: the older he became, the more he looked like his father. Second: he, Manolo Olivar, was a coward. Third: everyone in the town of Arcangel expected him to grow up to be a famous bullfighter, like his father.

No one had to tell him these three things were true. He and everyone in the town of Arcangel knew the first and the last of these to be true. And the fact that he was a coward only he himself was aware of.

When he was almost nine, he grew three full inches.

All of a sudden, as if overnight, he seemed to change. He became very thin, his nose lengthened, his limbs became awkwardly long, like those of a boy twice his age.

On the streets people began to turn around and remark about his resemblance to his father.

"It's the eyes! He has exactly the same look in his eyes!"

"The same sad eyes."

"It's not only the sadness. There is something more. Juan Olivar had eyes like no other man I've ever seen."

"And now the boy has that look."

"He also has his father's thin, long nose. The same nose."

"His was the longest nose in Spain."

"Why shouldn't it have been? He was the bravest. And in a *torero*, a long nose means bravery."

"Even with a short nose Juan Olivar would have been the bravest."

"I don't agree! There has never been a brave torero with a short nose."

"You speak foolishly. I can name you a dozen . . ."

This would lead into a fight of words, and Manolo would no longer be interested. The fact was that he had a long nose, like his father, and it seemed that this was to be his badge of courage.

"Look at his face."

"Just like his father's. Always brooding."

"A gypsy's face."

"There is no gypsy blood in the Olivars."

"Yet the face is a gypsy's face. Long, thin and dark."

"He might grow even taller and thinner than his father."

"That would be bad. The bulls then would always look too small."

"If he grows very tall, they will make him fight the biggest bulls in Spain. Each time the people will want a bigger bull."

"Until he will be made to fight cathedrals, not bulls."

"They will make him fight seven-year-olds, weighing two tons."

"There are no cows today in Spain that can drop bulls that would weigh two tons."

"I can name you twenty *ganaderias* with seven-year-old bulls that would weigh two tons. Easily two tons."

"Name me one! Just one! A hundred years ago, yes. Not today."

And again there would be an argument that might last for hours, if not days.

"He's growing fast. How old is he this year?"

"Don't worry, he will be twelve soon enough."

"Give him time. He is only a boy."

"So was Juan Olivar. At twelve one is not a man. Even though one is a *matador*, one is not a man."

People always talked about Manolo on the streets.

They talked about him, not behind his back, but all around him, in front and alongside and behind, not caring at all if he was within earshot or even standing and listening to them. It was a habit of the people of Arcangel.

And there was a reason for it. There have always been five things that people fear: war, disease, flood, hunger, and death. And of these, death has always been feared the most.

In Spain, however, people have found a way of cheating death. They summon it to appear in the afternoon in the bull ring, and they make it face a man. Death—a fighting bull with horns as weapons—is killed by a bullfighter. And the people are there watching death being cheated of its right.

In Arcangel the people had had their very own killer of death, Juan Olivar. He had been their own hero and their magician. Juan Olivar made their dreams come true: victory of man over death. The old saying, "Today as yesterday, tomorrow as today, and always the same," was no longer true.

But one day their killer of death met a bull that would not be deprived of his right. And the people of Arcangel, robbed of their pride, deprived of their magician, lost their hero. And when they lost him, each day became exactly like the one that preceded it and the one that would follow it.

Now the town of Arcangel was waiting, for that hero had left them a son who was growing up to once again take arms against death. They were waiting for the son to be like his father.

2

No matter how hard he tried, Manolo could not remember his father. He had been only three when the bull, "Patatero," drove his right horn through his father's heart. He was three when, one afternoon, two deaths happened almost at the same instant: the death of his father, and the death of his killer, the bull.

What he himself could not remember, was the one thing the town of Arcangel did remember. The town not only remembered, it was alive with the legend of Juan Olivar. Its very existence seemed to depend on one man's fame, one man's glory, one man's death.

There was nothing else to set Arcangel apart from other small Spanish towns. Juan Olivar alive, and even more dead, had created a town that lived on his name.

Sometimes Manolo thought Arcangel must not have existed before his father. Everywhere he turned he found shrines to the memory of the man he did not remember. In people's homes pictures of his father were kept alongside those of the saints. In every café there was his father in hundreds of photographs and dozens of posters: fighting a bull, waiting for the bull's charge, standing over the bull he had killed.

In the main square of Arcangel a great statue of his father and a bull, taller than any building, looked down over the red rooftops. His father's lean hands held the *muleta*, the cloth carved in stone seemed to blow in the wind; his father's sad eyes sighted down the length of the sword at the lowered head of the bull.

Another statue, almost as tall, stood in the cemetery, marking his father's grave. That one did not have a bull. His father stood alone, very erect, very thin, against the sky. His eyes were raised and Manolo, standing on the ground, could not see if they were sad. In his father's right hand were a bull's hoof, tail, and two ears; in his left, he held a bouquet of flowers.

And then, there was the museum, a building that housed the legend's heritage. Here there were the books that told about his father and copies of all the articles people had written about him. There was a copy of the painting that hung in his own house: a great life-size painting of his father in the red-and-gold *traje de luces*. The one he wore the day he was killed. There was a poster that had once hung outside Arcangel's bull ring announcing his father's first *novillada* when he was thirteen.

And also, there, at one end of the building, at the very farthest end, was "Patatero's" head. Mounted. Almost alive. Frightening in its power: the neck very strong, the horns very long and sharp, the eyes open and mean.

Manolo remembered when the people of Arcangel had built the museum. They had built it brick by brick, each inhabitant in turn carrying one brick: a procession of sad-eyed people in black. They, perhaps only his mother, or maybe the people of the town, had made him stand and wait and watch. It had taken a whole day, and he had grown very tired and had fallen asleep because he was only four and did not yet know about pride.

And still they talked, endlessly, everywhere, about Juan Olivar. They talked about Manolo's grandfather too; but very rarely, because although he too had been a bullfighter, he had not been considered a very good one. His grandfather had not died in the bull ring; he had died in a fire that had swept the town; died saving his son, Juan. But while he lived, he had fought bulls. He had fought over a thousand of them, even more than his son, but he was not remembered except as Juan's father.

The father Manolo did not remember had become the one and only hero of the people of the town. They knew everything he had done and everything he had said. They knew how wide and how deep were his wounds. And they even knew, or at least claimed they knew, what he had thought.

Most of all they knew that Juan Olivar's destiny as a great bullfighter had been known from the very beginning, from his birth. They never tired talking of it. They repeated themselves again and again. And still everyone listened. And everyone added or took from the story as he saw it.

"He wasn't more than two hours old," someone would recall, "when Señora Olivar sent for Maria Alvar. . ."

"At that time Maria must have been a hundred and three. . ."

"The old gypsy was more than that, at least a hundred and fifteen."

"How old Maria Alvar was doesn't matter. Juan was barely born when the greatest gypsy fortuneteller who ever lived. . ."

"Some said that her power to see into the future so clearly came straight from the devil."

"Who knows!"

"There was a much greater gypsy fortuneteller in

Granada at the time!"

"Who? Flora? She was never as great as old Maria. Besides Maria taught Flora all she knew."

"Maria Alvar could look at a newborn baby, and without cards, without stars, without anything at all, she could tell you when the baby would walk, when it would talk, whether it would get sick or not, and how sick it would be. . ."

"When she saw Juan Olivar, she fell to her knees."

"I was there! When she did that, do you know what I thought? I thought that little Juan would grow up to be the Holy Father!"

"What did Maria say?"

"I remember it as if it were yesterday! Still on her knees, she looked at the tiny baby and crossed herself. 'At twelve, not before, but at twelve, the boy will bring great glory to Arcangel. It will be in the bull ring. He will fight, and he will kill his first bull. And he will go on killing bulls for as long as he lives. And this town will have Spain's greatest matador!'"

"She didn't say any more? Didn't she say anything at all about how Juan would not be interested in bull-fighting until he faced his first bull?"

"She said nothing about that."

"Someone told me she had said it."

"She said nothing more. I think she saw his death, but she said nothing. Just what I have told you. No more and no less."

"Count de la Casa was the first to believe the old

gypsy. He took Juan to bullfights with him all the time. And he wasn't discouraged when the boy showed no interest in playing at bullfighting."

"How many *corridas* did Juan Olivar see before his twelfth birthday?"

"Twenty-five maybe thirty."

"Less than that!"

"Couldn't have been less, maybe more, but not less."

"No matter. The Count would take the boy to see the bulls being fought, and the boy would just sit there, not even interested."

"The Count never doubted that Maria was right. He just waited for Juan Olivar to become twelve."

"How carefully the Count bred that bull for the boy!"

"He knew, the Count knew, that the boy deserved the best his ganaderia had to offer."

"And the boy's bull was called 'Castalon,' and he was one of the best the Count had ever bred."

After such a conversation, someone would almost always read a passage from Juan Olivar's biography, by the most famous of all bullfight critics, Alfonso Castillo:

"It was there, at the spring *tienta* of Count de la Casa, that Juan Olivar, twelve, made his first pass with a cape. He went into the ring with a three-year-old bull, and the bull was dead fourteen minutes after Juan Olivar made his very first pass. In those fourteen minutes, the boy fought the animal with rare grace, fine skill, and great courage. And the bull was dead of a sword that was placed as calmly and as beautifully as any sword that has ever reached the heart of a bull has ever been placed. At twelve, having never practiced, or even shown any interest in the corridas he had seen, Juan Olivar was a matador. And the gypsy's prophecy was fulfilled."

It did not matter to the people of Arcangel that there had been no similar prophecy made about Manolo.

"Your mother wouldn't let a gypsy into the house," someone had once said to him angrily. "Maria was dead by the time you were born, but Flora was still alive. And she wanted to come and see into your future, but your mother would have none of that."

"We might have needed a gypsy's prophecy," someone else had added, "if Manolo looked less like his father. But we all know that he looks exactly like his father. And we all know that he will be just like his father. Nobody in Arcangel believes otherwise."

When Manolo had first heard them say how very much he looked like his father, he had gone home and stood in front of the great oil painting. He had taken a mirror from his mother's dresser and had looked at his father and then at himself. It was true what they were saying. Especially about his nose. But if a person's nose is long and he is not brave, what then? Does having a long nose help one be brave?

It was, at nine, that he first knew for sure he was not brave. Two things happened both on the same day, to convince him of this.

Coming home from school that day the boys he was walking with spotted a mule-drawn wagon full of hay. One of the wheels had broken off and the driver of the wagon had gone to get help.

The other boys climbed to the top of the hay; then, screaming with excitement, they jumped down onto the grass that lined the street. It was a high jump, and watching them Manolo knew that he could never bring himself to jump down from such a great height.

"Manolo! It's your turn."

"Manolo hasn't jumped yet. Let him jump."

"What are you waiting for?"

He heard them shout to him and saw them wave, but he could not move. The top of the mountain of hay seemed to touch the sky.

Jaime, his best friend, whose brother, Juan, wanted to be a bullfighter, came and took Manolo by the arm.

"What's the matter with you?" he asked looking at Manolo very hard. "You're missing all the fun! It's almost like being a bird, like flying. And you haven't tried it yet."

Manolo could not say anything. His throat had tightened, and it was terribly dry.

"Come on," Jaime said, laughing and dragging Manolo behind.

"I don't . . . I don't want to jump," Manolo managed to say before they reached the wagon.

"But why not?" Jaime wanted to know. "Why don't you want to jump?"

At this moment the owner of the wagon appeared. The boys saw him at the same instant he saw them.

"Get off," the man shouted. He ran forward, a whip in his hand.

But the boys were already off. They were running down the street laughing and shouting back. They all ran but Manolo.

"Assassins! Vagabonds!" the man yelled waving his whip at the disappearing figures.

Manolo paid little attention.

Had the man not come, he thought, his friends would surely have discovered what he himself now knew: he had been afraid; he was a coward.

"You spilled my hay," the man went on. Manolo almost jumped. His attention turned to the man at last. "You boys spilled my hay all over the street! You scared my mule!"

"I'll put the hay back," Manolo offered, feeling more miserable than he had ever felt in his life.

"Be off, before I take the whip to you!" the man shouted bending down to pick up the scattered hay.

Manolo wished that the man would whip him. He deserved to be whipped for having been afraid.

"Please, let me help," Manolo insisted.

"All right, help me, then," the man said grudgingly.

As he picked up the hay and loaded it back on the wagon, Manolo thought that the top of it was not all that high. Even if it had been as high as he had imagined, he, the son of the bravest man who ever lived, had no right to have been afraid.

Afterward, walking very slowly towards his house, he tried to remember other times when he, not knowing it, had been afraid and had shown his fear. There was last summer. Everyone he knew had been swimming or at least learning. And he had not been. He had not learned because he was afraid. He had pretended he didn't want to go swimming. Actually he had been watching the others splash and laugh and duck under the water, and he had been jealous. Still he had not made any attempts to learn. Now he knew, now he was quite certain, that it was because he was a coward.

And then there was the business of the bicycle. He was probably the only boy in his school who didn't know how to ride a bicycle. He did not own one. But several of the boys who had bicycles were willing to lend them to those who did not. He had never even wanted to try. That too showed that he was a coward.

How could he have lived all his years without knowing that he was the biggest coward in the world, he wondered; he, the son of the bravest of men? His new knowledge made him feel quite sick. It seemed that he had always been afraid. All his life, always afraid, afraid of everything. But what could he do, knowing it? He would have to learn to hide it until, until he learned to be brave. And he must learn, he knew. He must begin immediately.

The moment he made this decision, the second incident happened. He was crossing the *plaza* and suddenly a great black mass was bearing straight at him, almost touching him with all its roaring speed. He jumped back from the car and fell down backwards into the gutter.

It was four in the afternoon in the plaza with his father's statue at its center. The men who were always sitting at the tables of the café were all there as usual. As he fell, he heard them laugh.

"Manolo! Steady there, boy!"

"Never jump back! Never!"

"Stand your ground!"

"Like your father! He never jumped back."

"Shame on you! You must promise never to do that again."

He got up, wanting to run away and hide forever. But they made him sit with them. They gave him ice cream, and they kept talking to him.

There were six men, all of them *aficionados*, all of them followers of his father's career. Six men in black suits and white shirts, looking very much alike, thinking very much alike, talking very much alike. Six men who knew everything about bullfighting and everything about Juan Olivar. Six men, among a townful of people, who were waiting for Juan Olivar's son to bring back the glory that Arcangel had once known.

Although he had known them for as long as he could remember, Manolo could not distinguish one from another. He knew that they had different names, and that their faces were not quite the same, and that they did not live together. But he always saw them together: talking, sitting, drinking, smoking, walking, and waiting. Six of them. Six, who had seen him scared; six who were uneasy now, because they had seen him run.

"We've left you alone too long, Manolo," one of them said.

"It's high time that you see for yourself how to act when something's running towards you."

"It's high time you saw your first bullfight."

"You'll sit with us at a *barrera*, and you will have your first lesson."

"Today!"

3

There was one hour before the start of the bullfight. During that hour the six men tried desperately to tell Manolo all they knew about bullfighting. But what they knew would have taken days to tell.

"It took four men to write the Gospels," one of them said, "but it only took one man to write down everything there is to know about bullfighting."

"You must read Alfonso Castillo's five-volume work, *Of Bulls and the Men Who Fought Them.*"

"The boy's too young to read Castillo."

"I read a lot," Manolo said timidly, not wanting

them to think that he was too young.

"For now, you'll just listen to us. Listen and learn."

"In ancient times, especially in Crete, the bull was bred for strength and bravery. Lions were known to fight those brave bulls. Later a man would match his agility against the strength of the bulls. But the bulls of ancient times were neither as fierce nor as big as those of Spain."

"At first, centuries ago, when bullfighting began to develop in Spain, it was a pastime for the noblemen only. Through careful breeding, the bulls developed their extraordinary bravery which is completely lacking in all species of bulls except those raised on our peninsula. As the bravery was bred into them, cowardice and tameness were bred out. And today there is as much resemblance between a brave bull and an ordinary bull as there is between a wolf and a lap dog."

"Later we will tell you how bulls differ. Each bull has his own peculiar characteristics. One day, seeing a bull enter the arena, at a glance you'll be able to tell, or sometimes maybe only guess, how he will conduct himself in the ring throughout the fight."

"It will take time, but you'll learn."

"You will learn how bulls differ and how you must play each, not only according to the rules of the *toreo*, but also according to the bull's deficiencies or advantages."

Did my father know? Manolo wondered. Had his

father known everything that he himself must yet learn? And as if reading his thoughts, one of the men said:

"When your father was your age, Count de la Casa had already taught him much. And what he did not learn from the Count, he learned from Alfonso Castillo, himself."

"I wish Castillo would come to Arcangel and talk with the boy."

"He won't do that. He won't see a bullfight, and he will not talk bulls to anyone. Not since Juan Olivar's death."

"We could write him."

"He would not answer."

"We're wasting time. The boy knows nothing yet, and he'll go into the bull ring like a tourist."

"Pitying the animal and shuddering at the sight of the *picador*."

They laughed, and then once more became serious.

"Once, *la fiesta brava* was a duel between a man and a beast. Today it is not an even contest. For one thing the bulls are much smaller."

"For another the bulls' horns are often shaved."

"We needn't tell the boy that. His bulls will not be shaved."

"What does shaving the horns mean?" Manolo asked.

"It's a crime some cowardly bullfighters are guilty of. They make the *ganaderos* file down the bull's horns so that when the animal charges the target he misses. A brave bull, before he is brought to the ring, has been fighting other bulls in the pasture. He knows how to use his horns, as a boxer knows how to use his fists. He aims and judges his aim by the length of his weapons. And when these weapons are shortened, he misses by exactly the distance he's been deprived of."

"He can still gore a bullfighter, but the goring will not be so bad as if the horns were untouched."

"Can you tell when the horns have been shaved?" Manolo asked shuddering.

"The tourists can't tell; they're the only ones who can't."

"But then," Manolo interrupted, "what do they do to the bullfighter who has them shaved?"

"They punish him with a fine. But the cowards who fight shaved bulls usually can well afford the money."

"Enough about that. As I was saying, today it's less a duel and more of an art. The bull still possesses strength and courage and his horns for weapons. The man needs no strength but a great deal of bravery and skill and grace. He offers his body to the charge of an animal weighing a thousand pounds. He must know how to divert that charge past his body. And at the moment of truth, when he must kill, he stands alone, exposing his breast to the horns. And should those horns move upward at the moment of truth, they will drive death into him. For a chest wound is almost always mortal."

"If he kills honestly, if there is no cheating, he exposes himself to the chest wound."

"But some do cheat. When they do, everyone knows; even the tourists can see that they cheat."

"Don't expect it to be an even contest. The bull must die. Only sometimes, very rarely, does the bull not die. If he lives after he enters the arena, it is for one of two reasons: either he has been too cowardly and, disgraced, will meet his death outside of the ring, or he has been so brave that both the bullfighter and the public wish to spare him to perpetuate that extraordinary bravery in his descendants."

"A man may live, but also he may die, for the same reasons. If he is brave, he may die; or if he is too cowardly, he may live, but live in shame. Or he may be just wounded, either because of his bravery or his lack of it."

"You must remember that courage is not enough. A bullfighter must know and understand the animal he faces. Each animal."

"Although there is so much to learn, Manolo, you will be learning about the most noble of all animals. There is no sight more beautiful in the animal kingdom than that of a full-grown bull in action. Its bravery, pride, majesty, and strength cannot be matched by any other animal."

The six men cared much more for the animals than for the men who fought them, that much Manolo could see. As for the rest, his head whirled from the confusion that all the facts left. The voices of the men seemed to merge into one ever more insistent voice.

"Aficionados are divided into three groups. There are the tourists who know nothing, or next to nothing. They don't have to be foreigners, they can be Spaniards who go to corridas once or twice in a lifetime. Don't listen to them, everything they say is wrong. Then there are the *toreristas*. All they care about are the bullfighters. Some like the ones who look pretty in their traje de luces; some like the ones with fancy, flashy passes, worthless because they show neither skill nor courage. And finally, there are *toristas*, like us, bull fans. We appreciate only the pure artistry; the capacity of the bull and the way his actions affect the bullfighter's skill. Since the death of your father, there has been precious little for us to see. Bullfighting is dying. And it needs someone to make it come alive again."

Six pairs of eyes looked at Manolo. He felt that in each pair there was the same hope: that he, Manolo Olivar, would one day bring back to bullfighting the art of his father. And he lowered his eyes, afraid and ashamed, for he felt that their hope would never be realized.

4

They walked into the bull ring in the bright daylight of five o'clock. It was not the crowd that Manolo first saw, but the great ring of sand, half light, half dark. Empty. Quiet. And then he saw the people. The crowd was colorful, loud, waiting. From them there was no escape for anyone, Manolo thought, unless it was into the tranquil smoothness of the sand. And before he even sat down he decided that if his father had ever been afraid, it had not been of fighting a bull but of that ring of waiting people.

Manolo was seated between the six men, surrounded

by them, with two of them at each side of him and
two behind. He felt a gripping in the pit of his
stomach and a tightness in his throat; he hoped that
this time it was not fear but excitement. He concen-
trated, listening to the men, learning from them what
it was that he was about to witness. And hoping they
would not know, not today at least, how impossible
it was for him, Manolo Olivar, to ever be anything
like his father.

"Don't waste your pity on the bull."

"He will fight for his life, and he will die in battle.
And that's how he'd choose his death if he had a
chance to choose: in hot blood and not in the miserable slaughterhouse where he can't fight back."

"And don't pity the horses. It's a necessary and
ugly evil."

"The bull must hit something solid or he will not
go for the lure of the muleta. And he must be weak-
ened to lower his head. That's what the horse and the
picador are for."

"But remember that it's the bull that is most important. Watch its every move. He is the orchestra; the
bullfighter is only the conductor."

"The man must stand his ground. He must not run
away as you did from the car."

"The man must do three things: *mandar*, *templar*,
and *parar*. He must dominate the bull, hold his attention; he must have timing and rhythm, move the lure
just in front of the horns without permitting the bull

to reach it; he must stand his ground, keep his feet from moving in front of the bull."

"Unless the man is doing all this, he cannot command."

"The bull attacks by instinct. He attacks the cape and the muleta not because of their color but because of their movement. It is the man who must direct the cloth in such a way as to make the bull want to attack the lure over and over again."

Manolo heard the sound of the trumpet and then of the *paso-doble* being played. When they told him to look straight ahead, it was beginning. The crowd had become still and only the music played on as they came out, the men and the horses. First a man on horseback.

"The *alguacil*, he is the go-between, the president's man on the ground. He catches the ring that opens the *toril*, the gate from which the bull will come."

Then came the three toreros, each with his dress cape over his left shoulder and tightly wrapped around his waist, his left hand across his breast, the right swinging free.

"The oldest one, not in age but in years as matador, always walks on the right. The youngest in the middle."

"They have all had their *alternativas*, they are full-fledged matadors; for this is a corrida with full-grown bulls."

"Each man will fight two bulls."

"Unless the bulls decide otherwise."

The bullfighters looked very grave. For a moment Manolo thought hopefully that they were afraid. But there was no fear on their faces, just a sort of grave sadness.

"Behind each torero are his *banderilleros* and behind them the picadors."

"The men who work for a bullfighter are part of his *cuadrilla*. Each man's sword boy is waiting for him right below us. See."

Yes, he saw three men unfurling capes, throwing them across the wooden barrier that ran around the ring. But it was coming closer, the solemn procession, and at the end of it were withered old men, looking as if they were walking behind the bullfighters' hearse.

"Those are *mono sabios*, the men who clean the ring."

"And also, very often save the bullfighters' lives."

And there were others; Manolo was told they were the carpenters and those who would drive the mules that would drag behind them the dead bulls.

"The banderilleros can only wear black or silver embroidered suits. That's how you can tell them apart from the bullfighters."

"Later you can tell them apart by their clumsiness and their fear."

"Not always. Some bullfighters have more of that than their helpers." One of the men laughed, and then they all laughed. Meanwhile the procession reached the barrera, right below, and like a wave, broke.

"Each man must salute the president."

The three toreros looked up, towards the box where the president of the bull ring was seated; and each, not taking his *montera* off but pressing it down, acknowledged the man's presence.

Then before Manolo knew what had happened, the oldest bullfighter had thrown his dress cape up at him. The men beside him looked delighted. They almost shouted that the bullfighter, Emilio Juarez, had fought with his father many times, had recognized Manolo and was honoring him by presenting him with the cape. Manolo touched it gently. It felt silky and was richly embroidered. His examination of it stopped short as the man on his right jabbed an elbow into him:

"Now! Now it begins!"

"The toril!"

"Watch the gate of fear."

The bugle blew, and Manolo looked as the gate slowly swung open. There was nothing but a pitch-black hole. Suddenly something moved and sprang out into the arena; it was his very first bull that he saw! Black and angry and running, moving swiftly over the earth with his great body and shining with silver-black muscles. Manolo's heart came to a standstill at the sight of it.

"A calf!" The man at his side spat and then whistled with the others in anger, disappointment making his face ugly. If that's a calf, Manolo thought, I'd like to see his mother. He smiled to himself at this private joke.

Halfway round the ring, the bull caught sight of the magenta-and-yellow cape held out to him.

"That's one of Emilio's banderilleros. And there is the other."

The bull charged straight at the cape, which lay in waiting on the sand and was taken away before his horns drove into it.

"He charged well. Straight and true, but it's too early to know if he has any defects. Few bulls run as if they are on rails. Some do charge straight each time, but most hook and swerve, or break, or lean in, or prefer one horn to the other."

The bull charged straight again.

"He looks good. If he is, then it's because he has inherited his mother's courage and gallantry. But his beauty comes from his father. The father was not a big bull."

And now the oldest bullfighter, Emilio Juarez, came out from behind the barrier. Manolo watched him walk slowly toward the bull, which had already seen him and was thundering toward him. The blackness approached, running straight at him, and the man seemed unaware of the coming of horned death. He stood very straight and proud and unconcerned, holding the cape easily in his two hands.

"He will take him very close."

As the bull reached the cape, the man swung it alongside, slowly. The horns seemed to graze the man's thighs and the bull's rump pressed against the man's chest; for a moment the two were one, and the *olés* were loud, as loud as the beating of Manolo's heart. Again and again, the three—the bull, the cape, and the man—flowed past. Saliva ran in the wind from the bull's closed mouth, and the veins on the man's neck were gray and big like fingers. Seeing those veins, Manolo knew without being told that what looked so very easy was terribly hard. And after the fifth pass the man gathered the cape around him and brought the animal to a sharp stop behind his back.

"The easier it looks, the harder it is to do."

"That's a series of *veronicas* you've just seen and a fine *media veronica* ending it."

Manolo's eyes were on the beautiful animal in front of him. The blackness that was his strong body was glistening and heaving. His flanks were wet and his weapons, the horns, were curved and ended in a needle of danger.

"You should have seen your father do a veronica."

As they were talking, Emilio Juarez again cited the bull, this time with a triumphant: *"Ehe, toro!"* The animal lunged from his brief rest, and again man and bull became one in another series of veronicas. They danced through the emotions of fear and courage, fear evident in the crowd's *olés*, and courage in the movements of both man and animal. Manolo was fascinated by this dance. He watched, breathless, the magic that was performed in front of him; and when it was over, when the bull and the man stopped, he suddenly knew that he wanted to be able to do just that, to be a knight in the shiny suit of glory, to have people scream their praise and their fear for him. And for the first time that day, he was happy to be what he was, happy that the future he had feared so much was to hold so much beauty.

"Wasn't he very, very good?" Manolo asked.

"Yes, Manolo, luck was with you. You have seen your first bull and your first veronicas, and they were both very good."

"But the bull is a calf, you said."

"It is small and therefore less dangerous than a large animal, but still it is a beautiful bull to play."

When he looked again, he felt sick at what he saw. The bull had charged one of the horses, and the picador had driven a lance into the bull. Blood was running down the bull's side. Yet he did not make a sound; he kept pushing against the horse and against the weapon that was cutting down his strength. And Manolo lowered his eyes, for the pain seemed to be his own.

"It does the bull more good than harm. It is hitting something solid for a change."

But it must hurt him terribly, Manolo wanted to

shout. How could the bull endure it.

"The wound will never hurt him. By the time it begins to hurt, he will no longer be able to feel anything."

He saw the bull being taken away from the horse. The bullfighter played him skillfully with slow passes of the cape; the man wound up in the cloth, the animal following, bravely; the two not inches apart.

"Are you watching the *chicuelinas*?" Manolo was poked in the ribs. He was watching, and it looked quiet and beautiful, this dance of death. But then the sun caught the blood spurting from the deep wound, and again he wanted to cry out for the bull and his pain.

Now, once again, the bull headed for the punishment of the lance, headed straight and fearless for the pain. And Manolo knew that it was from the bulls that he must learn courage. More from them than from the bullfighters, for the bulls' bravery knows no limit.

Three times the bull went in for the pic, and now there were *olés* from the people that were meant for the animal.

"A *toro de bandera*. A truly brave little bull," they said.

When the bull moved into the shade, the blood was no longer red, just wet. The ballooning cape seemed now to hold him suspended. He knows he's dying, Manolo thought: he is preparing to die as gracefully and bravely as the people want him to die. And Manolo wanted to run to the bull and put his arms around his bleeding neck and protect him from further hurt.

"Emilio is going to place the banderillas himself," one of the men said. And when the man cited, the bull ran towards another hurt, barbed sticks. But now Manolo also felt frightened for the man who stood alone in the center of the ring, his legs in the dark shade, his head in the sunlight, awaiting the charge with just two sticks for protection. There is death for this man, Manolo thought. The bull ran forward and seemed to have finally hit the man. Yet he missed, and the man walked away, slowly, from the animal that for a brief moment only was aware of the hooks that were implanted in him.

"With the banderillas you watch for four things: how straight the man's body is, how he places the sticks, how close to the horns he gets while doing it, and how high his arms are raised."

Did the men expect him to remember all that, Manolo wondered. He hoped that they would not ask him questions to see how much he had learned.

Now Emilio Juarez came back into the *callejon*, the passageway between the seats and the ring. He was withdrawing the sword from its case, held by his sword boy, and taking up the red muleta.

"He will now dedicate the bull."

Emilio Juarez came into the arena, the montera in

his hands. He bowed to the president and then he looked straight at Manolo, his hat raised towards the boy.

"I dedicate this noble animal to you, the son of Juan Olivar. May his bravery teach you things a man's courage cannot teach you."

"Catch it," one of the men whispered.

The bullfighter turned around and threw his hat, from behind, toward Manolo, who caught it as all the people in the bull ring watched his flushed face.

"It's a great honor," one of the men said.

"What should I do?" Manolo whispered, excited by this completely unexpected attention.

"If you were older, you would be expected to present the bullfighter with a gift."

"Just hold on to it until the end of the fight and hope that he will make the dedication come true."

Manolo held on to the velvet-fur material of the hat, praying now for the man and for the bull, for their mutual bravery to teach him the length and breadth of pride and courage.

The men were telling him about the importance of the *faena*, the last part of the corrida. The man is alone in the arena; there is nothing but the man, the bull, the red muleta, and the sword it hides. The bull's fate and man's fate are at stake.

"With the muleta, there is only half the target, it's half as large as the cape."

"When the man holds it in his left hand, the target

becomes even smaller."

"It is only now that the man will look death straight in the eye."

He watched, holding his breath, as Emilio Juarez left his body exposed giving the bull his choice; either the body or the small piece of cloth. And yet, the bull, thanks to the infinite skill of the man, did make the choice of the cloth.

Manolo wanted desperately to know how it was possible for a man to play with a bull that no longer seemed dying but was using his horns to search for death. With each pass the bullfighter seemed to be hypnotizing himself into more bravery; and the stillness was interrupted by shouts of *olé*; and Manolo, himself, unaware, shouted also, his face feverish with excitement.

And then it happened. The man invaded the bull's terrain too deeply and he was on the bull's horns, being tossed up in the air, his legs and arms like a doll's, limp and falling. Manolo screamed out his fear at the instant the bull's horns caught. But the man landed miraculously on his feet.

"Luck was with him."

"But he should have known about the bull's *quarencia*."

"We shall teach you about the bull's terrain and the man's . . ."

But Manolo was not listening to them any more. It was incredible to him that the man could resume his passes after what seemed to be his death. His helpers ran out to his aid, but he pulled himself erect, proudly motioning them back and offering himself again to the bull's attack.

"The moment of truth!"

"The kill!"

Manolo saw the bull standing, its tired head down, its legs swaying a little, very thin, like sticks, the blood still pumping out of his withers. Emilio Juarez profiled, raised the sword to his eyes, and moved forward, toward the lowered horns. It seemed as if he was inside those horns; and then there was no more sword, its red hilt rose from the powerful neck of the bull. The man's left hand guided the animal slowly past him; and before the man's body reached the bull's back, the animal crumpled down, first to its knees, and then to its side. Death came over him very fast. It came before the other men who ran out reached him, before one of them struck a short knife into his nerve center.

What Manolo thought had been a lifetime had lasted only twenty minutes.

Then it was over; they dragged the bull out, his ears and tail cut off, as the crowd shouted and waved white handkerchiefs. Manolo scarcely listened to the six men telling him about the splendid kill. He was terrorized again by thoughts of the future. And his terror was for other bulls, other bullfighters, and for himself.

And at that time, at the time of his terror, a photographer's bulb went off. In one of the cafés there was a picture of his father, taken in the stands when he was eight or nine. But his father's eyes were grave and sad, not full of fear.

5

That began it. After that, at least twice a month, he was taken to a bullfight. On Sundays to Cordova or sometimes to Seville; and on Thursdays, if there was a fight in Arcangel, he would be back, seated on the same wooden seat, always the same seat, where he had sat that very first time. And always there were the men.

Sometimes, very rarely, there were only two of them; most often there were six, the men in black suits and white shirts stained with sweat.

"Today don't watch anything but the bullfighter's

feet. Look how solidly planted they are. See! He has all his weight on both feet. If the bull should brush lightly against him, he would not lose his balance."

Another time, "I don't want you to look at anything but the bull's charges. The minute the toril opens, watch to see if the bull will run straight out or whirl to one side. And when they throw the cape in front, watch which horn he favors."

And again, "With this bull all you should see is how he attacks the cape. Watch the man, the bull, and the cape, all three at the same time. Look at the man's hands. Do you see how he holds the cape, do you see the grip?"

"Today it's the kill. Watch them profile. Watch how high the bullfighters get up on their toes and how they sight down the length of the sword. The target is very small. You must aim carefully in order to kill properly."

He was learning; he was learning because he knew that his very life would depend one day on knowing. He was memorizing passes and remembering hundreds of facts and dozens of rules. He was taught how to distinguish stupidity from courage and flashiness from art. He was a good student; and the men knew it and were happy about it. But there were arguments.

"I'll get him a cape tomorrow."

"Not yet! He must not touch a cape. It must be like his father."

"But a cape! Let the boy play, practice what he's learning. I wouldn't give him a muleta, but a cape! What harm in letting him start with the cape?"

"At twelve. With the bull. For the first time."

"Like his father. Everything must be like his father."

"But there was no prophecy about *him!* We should do everything we can to help the boy."

"No!"

The argument was familiar. He had heard it before; almost since he could remember anything at all, it had been the same argument. They had tried to give him a handkerchief at four, then a tablecloth, later a man's jacket, and always there had been the argument. It had to be just like his father. For the first time with the bull. Not until he was twelve. Neither he nor they were to know if there was any talent in him, if his hands, like his father's, were born for the art of bullfighting.

Again and again they told him:

"A bullfighter must have courage, skill, and grace. And of these courage is the most important."

"Cowardly bullfighters are rare. Cagancho and El Gallo were two. But they had nerve instead of courage. When they wanted to, when they felt like it, their nerve could be mistaken for courage. They both had skill and grace; they were brave, but brave without the pride that turns bravery into courage. They were both gypsies, and they fought like gypsies, sometimes splendidly and sometimes not at all."

"Remember, Manolo, that it is not possible for a man to fight well without fighting bravely. Although it is quite possible for a man to fight badly and bravely."

"You can always spot cowardice. There is no place a man can hide it."

It was true. Many times he saw fear written very clearly on the faces of men who came to fight bulls and stayed to be hooted, their shame weighing them down, making their eyes desperate. And Manolo again and again swore to himself that he would rather die than show his own terror.

But the more bullfights he saw, the more impossible it seemed to him that he would ever be able to meet a bull alone, play it, and then kill it; especially kill it.

At first, after he started going to bullfights, he hoped that his mother would not let him be a bull-fighter. But that hope soon vanished. He overheard his mother one day talking to his aunt.

"It is his fate. I had a broken heart when he was born a boy."

"We had all prayed that you might have a girl."

"God willed it otherwise. It cannot be helped. Manolo will have to go and face the animal when the time comes."

Ever since they had taken him to his first bullfight, his mother's face had acquired a new sadness. She would hold him to her breast longer as she was saying goodnight, and he would hear her sigh, and sometimes cry, at night.

"You must be grateful," she would say to him, "to the men who do so very much for you. They are teaching you all they know, and they know more than any one else in Spain about *la fiesta brava*. They have always been very good to us. When your father died they were the ones who came and told me that I would never have to worry about money, not as long as we both were alive. Your father did make a lot of money, but like all bullfighters, before and since, he spent almost all of it. That's what people expect of bullfighters, generosity and foolishness. But he left us friends, and they have been helping us each year. Each year those six men give us something. And now they are giving their time to you. You must be grateful."

He was grateful. He had even begun to like them in spite of their impatience with him and their shouts of anger and their always-present cigars. They were good men, and all they wanted from him was to make their dreams come true. But that was the one thing he was certain he could not do for them.

That was the reason he began to practice. Manolo knew he could not possibly remember all that he had been told, but he felt he must not disappoint them completely. Even though he might die of fright, he would know how to move, what to do with the lure, how at least to pretend that he was, at twelve, a little like his father had been.

He found a cape and a muleta. Not his father's, because they were in the museum, but his grandfather's. They were folded in a box, kept in the closet. They lay in mothballs with a few photographs taken at small bull rings. Manolo felt sorry because in those photographs there seemed to be very few people in the stands watching his grandfather. There were also a few handbills announcing his fights, and that was all that remained of his grandfather's career as a bull-fighter.

Manolo practiced at night, after his mother had fallen asleep and could not hear him. He had to open the windows wide to clear the room of the smell of mothballs. And he did not dare even light a candle, but would swing the cape, much too heavy for his hands, in the light of the moon. He tried to make it float, effortlessly, in front of an imaginary bull. He tried to remember about the slowness and the control and the way he was supposed to command. At first, he knew he was doing everything wrong; and when, after a few weeks, he thought he did a veronica right, he could hardly control his shouts of joy and triumph.

He would worry in the morning. Then his eyes were red and his head so full of sleep he could hardly keep it from falling down on his desk in school. He would worry about being discovered.

The night that he decided to do fancy passes with the cape, the *quites*, and found that they were much easier to perform than the veronicas, he smiled to himself for the first time. He decided to practice all the passes the bullfighters do while taking the bull away from the horse. These were the passes with which they tried to outshine each other: the chicuelinas, the *gaoneras*, the *reboleras*, the *mariposas*.

He loved to watch the cape balloon gaily. For weeks he felt truly pleased at his mastery of these passes. But then, one day, during a fight when he expressed admiration for a torero who did them well, one of the men said:

"You don't need to learn the fancy passes. They're not necessary; you won't need them at all. You can take the bull away from the horse with a series of veronicas. Your father always did. He did veronicas and medias with the cape and *naturales* and *pases de pecho* with the muleta. Just four. Just four, and he was the greatest. And he killed! Oh, how he killed! Better than anyone before or since."

After that Manolo did not smile any more at night. He just practiced harder the hardest of all passes, the ones his father did so well. The veronicas and the medias were hard enough, because they required purity. But the muleta! He despaired of ever being able to master the red rug. Anyone, he thought, can swing a cape and make others believe he is doing it right, but how does one make the muleta look right? There was no body to it, no shape. It hung lifeless from his fingers. It fought him back, not surrendering like the cape, but making him feel ridiculous. And how was he going to amount to anything without being good with the muleta? After all, it was the *faena*, the last part of the fight, that was most important. The faena, and of course the kill.

But to kill! He still did not understand how brave men could stretch their courage to that point. He could not believe that he himself could ever be capable of killing a bull, he who could hardly watch a fly being killed without feeling its pain, its loss. But he found a stick, as long and straight as a sword, and he devised a way of practicing the kill. He placed a sock in the crack of an open drawer and with the stick, held the way bullfighters hold their swords, he launched at the sock, until he was able to hit it. He allowed himself no more than a square inch for his target. He tried to profile well, raising on his toes and going in straight and steady at the drawer, seeing nothing but the sock, white in the moonlight and almost invisible on dark nights.

Time passed very fast. And he began to gain confidence, began to believe in himself. He even began to think that the dream the men had of his being as great a bullfighter as his father was not so far-fetched after all. That's how he thought on days when he was happy. On other occasions he doubted everything. And then he would practice harder. He would do other things that he hoped would help him. He would walk close to cars, but he was always too afraid to get as close as he wished, although he taught himself never to back away from them. He bought a small rubber ball, which he kept almost always in his right hand.

"My brother Juan always keeps a ball in his right hand," his friend Jaime had told him. "He found out that that is the very best way to strengthen the sword hand. If you keep squeezing it all the time, your hand will become strong and steady for the sword."

Manolo never walked now. Instead he ran; and more often than not, he ran backwards, rather than forwards, because that was the way, Jaime's brother worked to strengthen his leg muscles. And Manolo found a tree overhanging the river and made himself jump. He still did not know how to swim, but he learned to paddle to shore after he had thrown himself from the height of the branch into space.

He did all this alone and in secret, afraid of being discovered. He still knew that he was a coward, but he also knew that he was working at overcoming his cowardice.

At ten, like everyone else in Arcangel, Manolo Olivar was waiting for the day, when, in two years, he would face his first bull. Like his father.

6

Count de la Casa lived in France most of the year. He only came to Spain early each spring for his annual tienta. The Count was an old man, almost seventy. Tall and very straight of posture, he always seemed to carry his thin body very carefully, as if he felt that it was an extremely fragile thing. He had close-set black eyes with pinpoints of fire in the middle of the pupils.

Each year when he came to Arcangel, a few days before the tienta, he summoned Manolo. They met in a café that was more a shrine to Juan Olivar than

it was a restaurant or bar. When Manolo was small,
his mother had taken him there. Now at ten, he went
alone. He did not have to be reminded this time to
put on a clean shirt and to wet down his hair. This
year he was almost eager to see the old man. He
wanted to ask him some questions, mostly about the
testing of the animals. And also, he wanted to find out
what was expected of him. He knew that it was most
unusual to fight and to kill a bull during the tienta, for
only cows were tested on foot; bulls were tested from
horseback. Because of the gypsy's prophecy, the
Count had had a bull waiting for his father. But possibly for him, for Manolo, he would only have a
small cow to play with. If he were not expected to
kill a bull, he thought hopefully, he might not disappoint them after all. He might be almost as good
as his father was that first time.

The meeting followed a long-established ritual.
They first shook hands.

"*Que tal*, Manolo? How are you?" The Count's
voice had not changed; it was still a harsh sound
coming from the very depths of his thin body. His
hands were like thin paper, and Manolo's own felt
big and clammy.

"Come along," the Count said, taking Manolo's
arm and leading him towards the bar. "What will you
have, *manzanilla?*"

Manolo shook his head.

"Oh, I forgot!" the Count said chuckling. "The

young man will have a soda," he said to the bartender.

The Count held on to Manolo's arm as they waited for the drinks, and asked how old he was this year. The drinks arrived.

"To all the brave bulls!" the Count said raising his glass and clicking it against Manolo's.

It was always like this. Every word was the same, every gesture repeated, year after year.

"And how old did you say you are this year?"

Manolo, quite warm in the discomfort of being with the Count, swallowed the sweet, heavy, liquid and replied looking down. He liked to look down at the floor where pink shells of shrimp lay uncrushed, mixed with sawdust.

"How are you doing in school?"

"Fine," Manolo replied beginning to make a mound of shrimp shells with his foot.

"And your mother, Señora Olivar, how is she?"

"She is very well, thank you." With the other foot Manolo pushed the sawdust into another mound. This way, with his feet busy, his eyes could be averted from the Count and the feeling of terrible uneasiness was bearable.

The annual testing of the bulls came in April, and Manolo's birthday was not until August. He was certain that they would wait until he was really twelve, going on thirteen, before he had to go to the Count's tienta. And so, when the Count asked him again how old he was, he answered, looking at the two neat mounds of shrimp shells and sawdust:

"I will not be twelve until the August after next."

"Oh!" The Count was surprised. He took a large swallow of wine, and Manolo, lifting his head, saw disappointment on the old man's face. He shouldn't be surprised, Manolo thought angrily. He knows very well when I was born; he knows that I will not be twelve for another year and a half. They all know it. Surely they won't make me fight before I am really twelve. The thought came like a nightmare. It had been all their decision, he thought desperately, for him to do everything like his father. His father had been twelve and not eleven. At twelve, perhaps he, too, would be ready.

"The boy has grown a lot this year. He saw his twenty-fifth corrida last Sunday." It was one of the six men, who were always there during these annual meetings. He had turned towards the Count and had said that.

"And how do you like them?" the Count asked Manolo. "How do you like the corridas you see?"

"I like them very much. Most of the time." He was happy at this change of subject. They were not going to make him do anything differently from his father. He would still have time, a whole year and a half, two years really.

"And when you don't like them, why is that?" the old man asked.

"I don't like them much," Manolo said softly so

that the six men would not hear him, "when the bulls are cowardly or treacherous or when the toreros are bad."

The count laughed, the sudden short laugh of an old man.

"If he is to be as great as his father, let him start a little earlier. Next year." Again one of the six men, Manolo did not see which one, said this loud and clear, breaking the silence in the café that followed the Count's laugh.

"What do you think?" The Count placed his arm on Manolo's shoulder as the boy kicked at the mound of sawdust with disgust. "Do you think you will be as great as your father?"

Manolo sighed with relief. The Count had ignored the busybody. Everything would be all right.

"Will you be as great as your father?" the Count repeated.

"Anyone who says that he's as great as my father lies," Manolo said, hoping the answer would please the Count.

"Does that mean that you don't think you'll be ready to fight next year?"

"It does not mean that at all!" He shouted in great anger. It was no use, no use to please the Count, no use to ignore the fact that they had all decided, without his knowledge, to cheat him of one year of his life. "It means," he continued quietly, hating them now, crushing a shrimp shell under his heel and realizing that he was shattering his own hope, "that neither I, nor anyone else, will be as great as my father was."

"The boy could fight even this year."

"He is ready now."

"He is as tall as Juan was at twelve."

"He knows as much, maybe more, than his father did at his age."

"We've been teaching him. Almost every day, for over a year."

"No," the Count finally said. "No, next year is soon enough. Maybe too soon. But it shall be next year."

"You've picked the bull already, haven't you, señor?"

"Yes, I've picked the bull. It will be three years old next spring."

Oh, how he hated them! The six men and the Count; most of all the bull that had been picked for him! Just a few minutes ago everything had seemed fine. He had been willing to accept his fate, but now they had killed everything. Killed everything that was fine and good with their cunning and dishonesty.

When he left the café, he felt certain that the whole world was determined to get rid of him. The town, the six men, the Count, even his very own mother, wanted him dead even before his twelfth birthday. There was no hoping now that the animal could be just played with. He would have to kill it. They had all known it from the beginning. Only he had been stupid enough to hope that they would not make him do everything just like his father.

For the very first time in his life he wished that he had not been born the son of Juan Olivar. He wished that he had not been born a Spaniard. He wished that he had not been born at all.

7

The town of Arcangel has both a soul and a heart. Its soul is the bull ring, and its heart is the marketplace. Like most small towns in Andalusia, it is bordered on three sides by olive groves and on one side by the Guadalquivir river. The olive groves belong to Count de la Casa, and the river belongs to everyone.

There are no professional fishermen in Arcangel; but the men and the boys who fish the river, on a good day, catch enough to provide the whole town with fish. Whenever that happens, the market, just a block away from the plaza, becomes even noisier than usual. The bargaining and the laughter echo through the narrow streets, bouncing from house to house, an epidemic of sounds spreading from the stalls to the balconies and traveling upwards to the blue sky above.

The earth of Andalusia, where Arcangel lies, is part of the people who live not only on it, but with it, form part of it, seem to merge with it, to share with it their poverty and their joys, their struggles and their good luck.

The life of the people of Arcangel takes the rhythm of seed time and harvest. Fields stretch away, beyond the olive groves. They have been cultivated by generations of Andalusians who have plowed and sowed and harvested the vegetables and the wheat that grow meagerly in the ground that is tired of bearing.

At the end of the fields, not even a mile from the town of Arcangel, there are hills that refuse to be used. Stones spring from the earth, and only occasionally a sturdy tree or hardy bush will grow under the hot sun.

The sun is hot most of the year. It scorches the people and it scorches the earth for five months, from May to September. The sun is the joy and the sorrow of the people. It destroys their crops while it warms them with the heat they could not live without. And when the rains come, they are either a curse or a blessing. Sometimes the river floods, and the people lose their animals, their crops, and even their houses.

At other times the newly planted seeds are watered by the rain, and the people are thankful for its coming.

Like most people of Andalusia, the people of Arcangel are poor. But they are too proud to quarrel with their fate. Instead they make war against sadness with songs and dances, with laughter, and with joy at just being alive. That joy erupts like a volcano once a year during the three-day *fiesta*.

During the fiesta, Arcangel becomes a chaos of color and music. The people do not sleep and they do not work during those three days. Instead they play, they sing, they dance, they laugh. It always begins with the Mass and ends in a litter of paper, exhaustion, and dying music.

> *"Oh, what a feast there's going to be,*
> *And then, what hunger we shall see!"*

goes the old song that tells the truth about Spanish fiestas. People save and wait for it; and when it is over, they save and wait again.

March 25th, the feast of the Annunciation by Archangel Gabriel, the patron saint of Arcangel, begins the three-day madness. It was on the eve of the fiesta, that Manolo saw Count de la Casa. The year before he had spent the three days with the six men, with the noises of the fiesta only in the background. Together they had seen a series of three bull-fights featuring the best and most highly paid toreros of Spain. Together they had seen the bullfighters dress, eat, wait, fight. With them they had talked about bulls and about other bullfighters. Manolo had been excited by their proximity, by the glamour that surrounded them. They wore the best suits money could buy; their cars were shiny and new; there was pride evident in their faces; and their gestures were almost royal. But he had wondered about the strangeness of their eyes, the faraway, almost vacant look in them. He wondered if that strange detachment was due to their having witnessed so many killings in the bull ring or to the presence of fear. For there was a sense of fear about them, in whispers of the cuadrilla after the drawing of the bulls, in half-finished sentences, in darting looks. This foreboding of danger had dimmed, at least for Manolo, the glamour and deadened the din of applause surrounding the fighters of bulls.

This year, in his anger, Manolo wanted to avoid everything and anything that had to do with bullfighting. He spent most of his time during the fiesta with his friend Jaime García. They went to Mass together; and afterwards they followed the procession winding its way through the narrow streets of Arcangel. They walked solemnly in the long morning shadow cast by the statue of the Archangel Gabriel as it was being borne aloft by the strongest men of the town. In the early sunlight the candles burned dimly; yet they burned, as always during processions and in between; for the Spanish burn four thousand tons of candles each year to their saints. And in this light, the sun's and the candles', Manolo saw, as if for the first time, the faces of the people. Still solemn, for they would not start laughing until after honor had been paid their patron saint, the faces had the crude beauty of the landscape.

As the procession reached the church from which it had started, a woman began to sing a *saeta,* more a lament than a song—a confession, sad and beautiful. And from that sadness and the beauty of this lament, the fiesta took its cue. The town, suddenly, like a spring gushing from under a rock, flowed into song. The guitars began a race; the tambourines of the gypsies joined in; and the castanets, like a million clattering hoofs, lent their beat. Flamenco songs and the wails of the *cante hondo* were heard and would be heard until the very end—the third, exhausted night of the fiesta.

Manolo and Jaime wandered through the stalls that were set up along the riverbank. They tried their hands at the games of chance, the shooting gallery, and the ring-tossing. Each one won a prize, a box of candy. They ran through streets festooned with paper and balloons, bouncing into and out of the thick crowd in their Sunday best. They stopped to catch their breath, and when they did, they joined in the songs; and often they ran into a group dancing, and half-seriously, half-mockingly, they danced the flamenco, stomping their feet and chanting all the while, then clapping and laughing and running away again.

They spent their savings on ice cream and cotton candy and rushed home to get more money. Neither one, nor anyone else in Arcangel, was poor. Not during fiesta. They rediscovered the town, finding a ruin they had never known existed, and planned someday to establish a secret hideout there. They listened to the quarrels that erupted like brush fires and died as suddenly as they started. They stole apples from a cart and were chased with shouts by the vendor. They reeled against each other when they were laughing themselves into tears, and they stumbled against each other when they felt exhausted. They went to the outdoor movie twice and giggled when the cowboy kissed the girl and roared their approval at the appearance of the Indians. They climbed on the roof of a house and let homing pigeons out of their cages, all the while frightened by their daring and by the belief that the white specks would not come back from the sky before the loss was discovered by the owner.

For three days and three nights Manolo managed not to hear anyone speak of bullfighting. He managed to dodge the six men, although he did see them several times and thought they were looking for him. When the crowd surged towards the bull ring, the two boys fought against its current. When they saw the bullfighters' cars, they darted in the opposite direction without even giving the occupants a look.

For two weeks after the fiesta Manolo played ball with his friends after school and went back to studying in earnest; for his school work had suffered because of his preoccupation with bullfighting, his lack of sleep, and his lack of interest. For more than two weeks he did not think about the future, and he did not resume his nocturnal practicing.

And then, one day when he and Jaime were fishing, his friend brought up the subject.

"My brother Juan is going again to the pastures to cape the bulls." Jaime looked proudly at Manolo, who spat out a piece of grass he was chewing on. He had been afraid, during the fiesta and afterwards, that at any moment someone would remind him aloud of what he had not forgotten but wished he could forget. "He thinks he's going to be another Belmonte, that crazy brother of mine. You know, he read me Belmonte's story; how he used to look—skinny and all twisted up and hungry; and how he used to swim the Guadalquivir at night and cape the bulls on their pastures. He used to stand naked in the moonlight, and with his ugly little face and his ugly body he felt like God. Juan says that's exactly how he feels, too."

Their strings with worms barely moved with the moving water. The fish were not biting. Manolo began to chew on another piece of grass, hoping that Jaime would not continue talking about his brother.

"I am afraid for him," Jaime said with a sigh. "I know it's silly, because I can't do anything about it. I couldn't tell him not to poach on the pastures. But you know there are mean guards all over those places, and they have orders to shoot at anybody and everybody. They wouldn't ask any questions, they'd just pull the trigger. I'd hate for my brother to die of a bullet before he had his first real chance with the bulls. I do wish he'd let me come with him. I could act as his lookout."

"Have you asked him if he'd let you?"

"Of course. Many times."

"Can't your father stop him from going?"

"No. I don't think he would anyway. I am sure he knows about it, but since he, himself, as a boy used to do it . . ."

"I didn't know your father was a bullfighter."

"He was."

Jaime didn't seem to want to go on. All Manolo knew about Señor García was what people said around town. The boys' father hated everybody and hardly ever left his house. Their mother worked in the factory where they bottled olives, and it was she who supported the family. People said that García should be ashamed of himself for not lifting a finger to bring money into the house. But that's all Manolo had heard. He didn't know why Jaime's father hated people or why he wouldn't work. And he would not ask Jaime about this. He had never been invited inside Jaime's house, had never even talked with Juan who wanted to be a bullfighter. He had seen Juan a few times, but they had only nodded to each other.

"Why do the guards shoot at the boys who want to play with the bulls on the pasture?" he asked Jaime, suddenly wanting to hear more about this forbidden game.

"Once fought, a bull will attack a man rather than a lure. Besides the ganaderos are supposed to swear or something, when they are selling their bulls for the bull ring, that the bulls have never been fought on foot."

"It must be very difficult to fight bulls at night in an open field," Manolo said jiggling his line. What he really meant to ask was whether Juan was afraid of doing such a thing.

"Sure it's difficult. First you have to separate a bull from the herd so that he will attack your lure. In a herd the bulls just stand. They're sort of tame when they're together. But once you separate them, they're mad and want to kill."

"Your brother really does want to become a bull-fighter, doesn't he?"

"That's all he wants! That's all he talks about. That's all he ever dreams about."

Jaime had never talked with Manolo about the future that the town had planned for him. He felt Jaime must be well aware of the coming tienta. By now, since his encounter with the Count, he was sure everyone in Arcangel must know that it was to be next year: that a bull had been chosen for him. Manolo liked his friend for never bringing up the subject. Although at times he did want to talk about it, he knew he could not. To do so would be to confess her fears to his friend.

That night he lay awake, thinking about the future. He was also thinking of Juan out somewhere in the dark with a herd of bulls, the guards looking for him to shoot him down. If only he, Manolo, could be brave enough to try something like that. If only he could be out there with Juan testing his passes with an animal. But he was not like Belmonte, nor was he like Jaime's brother, nor was he brave like all the other boys who had ever wanted to be bullfighters.

He lay down on the bed and cried into the pillow, cried for the shame of his cowardice. He cried for a long time; and when he could cry no more, he made a decision. He was going to ask Jaime's brother to let him go along the next time he went to the pastures. He was going to face his first bull before the tienta! He had to know now if he had courage enough to face a bull. He could not go on living any longer without knowing if he was capable of conquering his fears. This would be a test. No matter how it came out, he would be able to sleep afterwards. He would know.

With that decision made, he got up and, taking the cape in his hands, began to do a series of veronicas, better than he had ever done them before, better than he had ever dared hope he could do them. And when the sun rose and the room became light, he was still at it, feeling a new art in his hands, a brand new strength in himself, and a confidence he had never known.

8

It was Sunday, and Manolo went to mass alone. After church he walked to Jaime's house. He had to ask for directions, and as usual people recognized him. The Garcías lived in the poorest part of Arcangel, in a crooked house that leaned against another. Before he reached Jaime's house, the news of his coming had spread, and Jaime was waiting for him outside.

"Manolo! What brings you here?" the boy wanted to know.

"Is your brother in?"

"What do you want with Juan?"

"I am sorry but I can't tell you. I'd like to talk to him."

"Come in, then. He's inside. But so is my father, and he doesn't like you."

"Why doesn't he like me? I've never even met your father."

"He doesn't like you because you're Juan Olivar's son."

"But why?"

Before Jaime could answer, his father appeared in the doorway. He was rather a short man, with hair that needed cutting and a chin that cried out for a shave. His eyes were small but extremely bright.

"Well, well, well," he sang out in a mocking voice. "The great son of a great father! And to what do we owe the honor of this visit?"

"Señor García," Manolo said bowing slightly.

"What other happiness can we expect after this?" the man said, throwing his arms in the air as if in joy. "Come in, come in, great son of a great father."

"Is he making fun of me?" Manolo whispered to Jaime, very uneasy about the man's strange behavior.

"He's just a little jealous," Jaime whispered back.

"Great son of the great Juan Olivar, won't you sit down?" The man pointed to an old upholstered chair that dominated the otherwise almost empty room.

"No, thank you. I just came to see your son, Juan."

"What possible business could you have with my idiot son?"

"It's rather private, and I would very much like to see him right away."

"He's still asleep. He has been to Seville. He caped some bulls in someone's pasture; and I believe," the man laughed bitterly, "he got hurt somewhat. But then, Juan does not get invited to tientas. But enough about him! You look exactly as your great father looked at your age. Are you too going to be the greatest torero Spain has ever seen?"

Manolo did not like being mocked by the man, and he did not know how he should answer him.

"Father, let him go to see Juan," Jaime said.

"Not yet! Not before we have our little talk," the man said turning to Manolo and pointing to the chair again. "Sit down, and I'll tell you a story."

Manolo did as he was told, more to humor the man than to hear what he had to say. He felt very uneasy; if it had not been for Jaime who remained in the room, he would have fled.

"You didn't know that I knew your father, did you?" The man laughed as Manolo shook his head. "I saw your father kill his first bull at the famous tienta of Count de la Casa. But I was not among those invited to see the young genius. I sneaked in and," he laughed again, "sat hidden on the branch of a tree. There I was," he pointed towards the ceiling, "hidden in a tree like a bird!"

"Why are you telling him this?" Jaime asked softly.

"Please go on," Manolo said, wanting now to know more about this man's relationship to his father.

"You see, Jaime, your friend is interested," the man said with a crooked smile. "Well, there I was like a bird, up in the tree, and there was your father, fighting his first bull. He never wanted to be a bull-fighter, or at least no one but that gypsy who prophesied great fame for him, would have guessed that he wanted to fight bulls. I, on the other hand, up there in the tree, had already caped a dozen bulls on the pastures and jumped into rings and been jailed for it. But I had not been invited, although I would willingly have given both arms and legs to be where your father was, in the ring with a bull of my own, making history.

"After that, your father and I went our separate ways. I always tried and never got anywhere, and he never seemed to try and got to be the *número uno* of all Spain. Oh, I fought bulls! Usually the ones that had already been fought a few times, the ones that never charge at anything but a body, bulls that had been taught 'latin' at night on their own pastures by boys like me, by boys like my son Juan. They never paid me for those suicides; but I kept hoping, stupidly, that the more horn wounds I got in my body, the faster I would be discovered by someone, and the sooner I would get a chance inside a real bull ring."

The man laughed again, and Manolo lowered his eyes in embarrassment.

"Well, that's how it went. I have eighteen wounds in me, one that goes clear from my knee to my thigh and doesn't end there because the same horn ripped open my back. I got that one two weeks after another horn caught my eye, the right one." He leaned towards Manolo and pointed to his eye. "I can't see out of it, but no one can tell that. Anyway, your father and I met again. He was by then a very famous torero. After those two wounds, I decided to ask him for a job as his banderillero. He had just lost one, killed by a bull, and he needed one. That's the reason I went to him and asked him for the job. He took me on. I stayed with him for almost a month. Not quite a month! And then," he laughed more bitterly, "I was fired! Fired because I failed to notice something out of that right eye of mine. Fired because Juan Olivar thought I had been drinking and was not doing my job."

"But he didn't know," Manolo said hurriedly. "He didn't know about your eye!"

"No. He didn't know. He didn't know about the eye. Nobody knew. If he had known, he would never have hired me. Still I was fired with nowhere to go, nothing to do, because all I knew was bulls and no one wanted a half-blind banderillero. And now, my boy Juan knows nothing but bulls. But will he become a bullfighter? No! He will never become a bullfighter. And even if I could, I would not lift a finger to help him. Do you know why? Because the cards are stacked against us. The Garcías are ill-fated. No gypsy needs to tell us that. And no gypsy needs to tell you that you were born lucky, that you'll become a bullfighter."

He got up from the edge of his chair, a broken man, in spirit as well as in body. There was something quite useless about his limbs; he was not a cripple, yet he moved as if he were; and Manolo felt sorry for him.

"Juan Olivar's son and not Miguel García's son will be a torero!" he cried, bitterness making his face ugly. "And what, oh great son of a great father, do you know about our great fiesta brava?"

He stood over Manolo, waiting for him to answer; and for the first time in his life, Manolo felt the pain of guilt. In a way, he thought, I am responsible for this man's broken dreams. Yet he did not know exactly how he could have been responsible.

"I hear," Señor García said, without bitterness now, as if the silence of the boy and his downcast eyes had mellowed him, "I hear that the Count has picked the bull for you, and that you are to fight it next spring."

"Yes."

"It will be exactly like your father's start. I imagine that the great Castillo will be there?"

"I don't think so."

"I am sure he will."

"Once, Castillo," Jaime interrupted very fast as if

afraid of being stopped by his father, "saw my father in a small bull ring. He wrote that he was a great killer. What exactly did Castillo say about you, father?"

"I've forgotten," the man said and his gloom returned. "And do you want to be a torero like your father?" He looked intently at Manolo.

"I don't know," Manolo said feeling miserable.

"Oh, you don't know? You don't even have *afición*, that Spanish poison which seeps into one's blood and makes an invalid out of the strongest of men? You don't even know anything about that afición that makes one wake up in the morning with one thought: to fight a bull, to go out and face an animal with death on his horns? You don't know what it is to forget one's family, one's health, even God? I knew a boy once who killed a woman. Do you know what he killed her for? For a chance at fighting a brave bull. The husband who arranged the killing was quite cheap: he gave the boy a bull that had been fought. And the boy was killed, too. But I don't think the boy minded. You see, no one else was willing to give him an animal to fight. If you do not know what afición can do, can make you do, then indeed you are a lucky boy."

"But I do have afición!" Manolo cried out.

"But you just said that you didn't know if you wanted to be a torero. Jaime, didn't he say that?"

"Leave him alone, father."

Manolo wanted to run away, but suddenly an idea
came to him. He could do something for this man to
make up in a small way for the things he, himself
had and the man had been deprived of.

"Señor García! It is because of my afición that I
came to see your son, Juan."

"Oh!"

"I . . ." Manolo smiled at the man, "I wanted to
know if he could come to the tienta with me." It was
not a lie. He hadn't come here to ask that, but now
that he had, he would see to it that Juan was invited.
He was sure that the Count would not mind.

The man looked at him unbelieving.

"I'll ask the Count if Juan can come along," Manolo
added. "And I will also ask him if Juan can make
some passes."

The man extended his trembling hand to Manolo.

"Would you really do that?" he asked trying to
hide the tears in his eyes. "Would you do that for
my son?"

"Manolo, that would be wonderful!" Jaime
shouted.

"All he needs," his father said softly now, "all he
needs is one chance. For someone to see him. I know
he would be very good. I just know it."

"Could I see Juan, now?" Manolo wanted to
know. He promised himself that he would not only
ask, but insist, that Juan García come with him to
the tienta.

Jaime took him into his brother's room. Juan was still asleep as they walked in. There was a black bruise extending from his hairline down his right cheek and around his right eye.

"He got tossed rather badly last night," Jaime said pulling the covers off his brother. "Wake up, Juan!"

Juan opened his eyes.

"Does it hurt?" Manolo asked. "Is your eye all right?"

Juan blinked, pushed back his hair, and then smiled at Manolo.

"Sure it's all right. I won't go blind like my old man. What are you doing here?"

"He's going to ask the Count if you can go to his tienta next year."

Juan sat up in bed.

"You're not joking, are you?"

"I'll try to get you an invitation," Manolo said, now feeling quite certain that he could. "I promise! You'll be there."

"You know," Juan was laughing, "I was going to sneak in and watch you from the same tree as my father watched your father."

"I want to talk to you about something else," Manolo said. "Jaime, could we talk alone?"

"Sure, if you don't trust me."

"It's not that; it's something private," Manolo said smiling.

"All right. Have your secrets," Jaime said pretending to be hurt.

When he had left the room, Juan wanted to know what the secret was.

"I thought—" Manolo didn't know how he should ask. "I thought . . ."

"Do you want me to teach you the capework?"

"No, it's not that. I thought that if you were going to . . . to cape some bulls in the pasture that maybe you could take me with you."

"You wouldn't want to do that." Juan said, rubbing his side. "It's too dangerous. If the bulls don't get you, there is always the guard. You don't need to take chances." He threw the covers off and jumped out of bed. Manolo saw a long scar on one of Juan's legs. "You are the son of Juan Olivar; and anytime you're ready to fight bulls, they'll have bulls ready for you."

"But . . . but I don't know if . . ."

"You don't know if you can do as well as your father did with his first bull? Without first practicing with an animal?"

"Yes."

"Don't worry, probably nobody could do as well as your father. Besides, you know that you're not supposed to know how to use the lures. Have you been practicing?"

"Yes."

Juan clucked his tongue and waved his finger in front of Manolo's nose.

"Shame on you." He laughed.

"You won't tell anyone?"

"Of course not, what do you take me for?"

"You see," Manolo said, feeling more at ease now with this boy who seemed to understand, "I don't want to make a great mess of things. I know I can't be as good as my father, but I don't want to disappoint them so much that they are ashamed of me."

"I'll tell you what we're going to do." Juan had put an old jacket on top of the shirt he slept in. "There is a small bull in the courtyard of the bull ring. It's there for tomorrow night's fight, the circus fight. We'll go tonight and cape him. All right?"

"That's wonderful!"

"I'll come by your house at about two o'clock in the morning."

"Thank you, thank you, Juan."

"Don't thank me. I should thank you for that promise."

"Do you know where I live?"

"Who in this town doesn't know the house of Juan Olivar?"

9

They were very careful not to be seen by anyone. Although it was past two o'clock in the morning, there were still many people on the streets. The two did not talk and walked a little apart from each other.

Manolo held on to his muleta, which he had hidden under his coat, and he felt his fingers trembling. If he had thought he knew the meaning of fear before, he was learning it all over again in the walk to the bull ring.

They had to wait in the shadows of a doorway until a couple of men passed the bull ring. Then they rushed toward the locked gate.

"We have to chin ourselves, and then crawl through that space," Juan whispered, pointing to about two feet of opening between the heavy wooden gate and the beginning of the stone wall above.

"Follow me," Juan said softly as he jumped up, grabbed the edge of the gate, and pulled himself up and then sideways until he disappeared. Manolo could not make it. He was a little shorter than Juan and not nearly so athletic. Juan reappeared at the top of the gate. Lying down, he extended a hand to Manolo, who managed to pull himself up. Together they jumped down and were safe inside the bull ring enclosure. Manolo looked back at the height from which they had jumped and smiled to himself. The wagon of hay, from which he had once been afraid to jump, had not been nearly so high.

"They will have the cows penned up all together in the big pen. So the bull that is meant for 'El Magnifico' must be in one of the smaller pens. It will be, I guess, no more than a two year old. But I'll bet 'El Magnifico' will have trouble with him. He was good once, before he got gored for the first time. Then after that goring, he seemed to lose his ability but not his nerve. Now when they book 'El Magnifico' to fight anywhere, it's just to show people how well he gets tossed by the animals. Come on, Manolo, we'd better get started."

They could barely see inside the structure of the

bull ring, passing by the infirmary, then the chapel, then the place where the horses waited, and the place where the dead bulls were butchered. Even though there had been no bullfight for two weeks, there was the smell of animals all around them.

"The pens are on the opposite side," Juan said. "We can cross over to them through the stands."

Suddenly they emerged into the moonlit bull ring, and there it was, the arena, empty. Manolo caught his breath. It looked so gigantic, like a sea, like a desert.

"Give me your muleta," Juan said. When Manolo handed it to him, Juan raced towards the sand, vaulted the barrier, and was inside the ring, taking off his coat. He had brought with him his "sword," a stick that was sanded down and painted silver. Now Juan began to make passes with the muleta, slowly, beautifully, as good as any Manolo had seen in the ring. As he watched the boy alone in the arena, Manolo knew that what he himself had achieved would never do. Juan had a feel for the red rag; he seemed to be able to breathe life into it. It obeyed the art of his hands and was part of his lithe body; he turned and it followed, effortlessly, the fluid lines of his movements. And Manolo was aware of something else. This boy loved very much what he was doing. He was citing the non-existent bull with soft words of command, and after finishing a series of left-handed passes, aware of their perfection, he shouted to himself, "*olé*." And then he looked up towards the empty stands, and Manolo saw how proud and how like a bullfighter he appeared. There was a smile of triumph on his face for a moment; then, as suddenly as it came, the smile disappeared and Juan looked sad.

"Let's go," Juan said.

"You're terribly good," Manolo managed to say.

"Oh," he shrugged his shoulders, "you should have seen me with the seed bull yesterday. I caped him with eighteen left-handed passes, and I, myself, knew I was as good as anyone."

"And he hurt you?"

"Slammed me down a couple of times before he knew what he was doing. He probably thought I was one of those silly amateurs. Hey, Manolo, don't you want to practice a few passes?"

"No," Manolo replied. He had not even stepped onto the sand; he felt unworthy of doing even that.

"All right, let's get to it," Juan said joining Manolo in the stands. They walked around until they came to the toril. "Let's go this way."

They could not see where they were going after they entered the dark passageway through which the bull had to walk to reach the ring.

I won't do it, I can't do it. Manolo groped his way behind Juan, wishing he were not there.

Juan stopped.

"If we find it, let me go in first. You don't mind, do you?"

"I don't mind," Manolo said, swallowing hard.

"Look," Juan seemed to have sensed the fear in Manolo, "you don't have to do it. No one is making you. If you don't want to play with the bull, don't. I will understand. Besides, I really think it would break all these people's hearts if you were to get hurt or anything."

They resumed their walk through the darkness, Juan feeling for a door, a latch, anything that might lead them to the pen. Manolo, very thankful for what had been said, breathed more easily. Again Juan stopped.

"I don't want you to think," he said softly, "that I am like some of the others. I know that I should not be poaching on someone else's bull. It is very danger-ous for a bullfighter to face an animal that has been played with. And that's why I won't give this animal any more than a couple of passes. And when I go to cape them on the pastures, I never touch any bull but the seed bull. They are never fought anyway. So you see, I have my code of honor." He laughed. "And if," he continued, "you feel like giving him a few passes, be sure it's just a few because I'd hate to think that we might be responsible for 'El Magnifico's' getting hurt."

"How long," Manolo asked, happy for this new delay, "how long does it take a bull to learn?"

"To learn to go for the man instead of the lure? About twenty minutes, or so they say. That's why the fights are never longer, or at least that part with the man and the bull alone. So you see, it's important not to play with this one long. And by the way," he said softly, "if I should get carried away, you shout to me to stop."

"And," Manolo's throat was again very dry, "what should I do if, if . . ."

"If the bull catches me and tosses me? Well, try your best to take it away from me until I can get up again."

"Of course," Manolo mumbled, ashamed of having asked, ashamed of not having known, and mostly ashamed because he felt that if anything were to happen to Juan he, Manolo, could not help him.

They heard the bull. It snorted, and they followed the sound.

"It must be here," Juan said stopping at a door made of planks of wood. He put his ear to them. "Yes. He's here! Now, listen. This opens from the top. It's on pulleys, so I'll try to lift the door up, but it might come down if I don't manage it all the way. Can you hold it while I am there?"

"But, if I hold it, I can't come to help you if . . . if anything happens."

"Don't worry about it."

"Let's not do it," he said, before he knew that he had wanted to say it.

"Not do it? But that's what we came for!"

"I only meant," Manolo trembled over the words, "I meant let's leave that door open in such a way that

I could get to you."

They could hear the bull now quite plainly; it was scraping the sand with its hoofs.

"Ready?" Juan asked.

"Wait," Manolo whispered. "What . . . what if the bull comes at us when we open this . . . this door?"

"He's young. And they're curious but not dumb at that age. He'll wait until he sees what's happening. He won't rush out. Or at least, that's what I am counting on. All right, ready now?"

"Ready."

Juan found the pulleys that opened the door. Slowly it lifted, and they could now hear the breathing of the animal. When there was two feet of space at the bottom, Juan tried to see if the door would come down. It did slide back.

"I'll have to use my jacket on one side and yours on the other," he said. He jammed the pulley ropes with the jackets, and now they were able to crawl through. "I'll go ahead; you just put your head through and watch. Then, when I'm through, you can cape him yourself," said Juan getting on his knee. "Aren't you going to wish me luck?" he asked, his face in the moonlight smiling at Manolo.

"Good luck," Manolo managed to say.

He bent down to see the boy scramble up, the muleta in the same hand as his "sword."

"*Ehe toro!*" Juan called softly, and moved to one side. Manolo saw the bull then: a black, glistening mass, white horns shining. It was big, much bigger than he had thought any bull could be.

"*Ehe toro!*" Juan repeated a little louder, shaking the muleta, now close, not more than five feet from the animal that stood still, waiting. And suddenly it charged, whirling at the boy. He'll get killed, Manolo thought; but Juan, without moving away, made the bull change its course. The animal followed the lure, which moved slowly a little ahead of his horns. He came back and again was taken smoothly, slowed down by the boy. Five times the animal and Juan seemed to touch, to be glued together, as Manolo watched. Then, standing straight, the boy turned his back to the animal and sent him away with a beautiful pase de pecho.

"Do you want to try?" Juan whispered to Manolo. "He's a good little bull." Juan stood not far from the bull, not looking at him, not afraid of the charge that might come.

"Watch out," Manolo shouted as the animal moved towards the boy. It did not catch Juan, however, who slowly, arrogantly, lifted the lure in both hands and let the animal charge under it. Back came the bull, and again, with quiet assurance, the boy controlled the animal's speed and direction. Without looking back, Juan walked towards Manolo. The animal seemed to have been nailed to the sand by the last pass, but suddenly it charged fast, too fast for Manolo to warn Juan. It happened in an instant. The boy was tossed up in the air and landed with a thud on the ground. The bull stomped the earth and moved his horns towards Juan, who had both arms thrown over his head. But Manolo was there. He acted automatically with no thought of what he was doing. He picked up the muleta and waved it in front of the horns, and the horns charged the red cloth. Manolo ran backwards, taking the bull away from Juan; he even screamed "*Ehe toro!*"

"It's all right," Juan shouted getting up. "I'm fine."

It was then that Manolo looked at the bull, as if for the first time. The horns were inches away, and the black eyes were staring at him. He was standing between Manolo and Juan's voice.

"Thanks a lot," Juan was saying, "but you better not play with him any longer. We should leave him alone for 'El Magnifico'."

Manolo felt sick. He had to hold his head high not to vomit right there.

"*Ehe toro!*" Juan came close to the bull, and the animal whirled and charged at the boy, who held no lure. Manolo watched horrified as Juan, dodging the horns, took the bull away. Without being aware of how he reached the opening, Manolo climbed through it and vomited his fear into the darkness.

He turned to see Juan letting down the planks.

"That was wonderful of you!" Juan said, his hand extended. "If it hadn't been for you, I would be lying there dead."

Maybe he did not notice, Manolo thought; maybe he didn't see that I was paralyzed, that I couldn't have moved. Maybe he doesn't know that I vomited. Maybe he didn't see any of this.

"It was good that you didn't play with him any longer," Juan said as they made their way through the lightless corridor. "If you had, and if something should happen to 'El Magnifico', you'd never forgive yourself; and something is bound to happen to that boy because he knows nothing about bulls and shouldn't even be allowed to fight this little one."

Little one? To Manolo it had been a gigantic bull! He realized that he had better say something or Juan would think that he was still paralyzed with fear.

"Why aren't you a bullfighter?" he managed to say, the words coming through his parched throat with difficulty.

"Are you joking?" Juan laughed. "It takes money or friends to become a bullfighter, and I have neither."

"But you're so good and so brave. You . . . you took that bull away without a cape or muleta."

"Oh that! That's called *al cuerpo limpio*, with just your body. I do that often. It's good practice, and it doesn't harm the bull at all. I do that on the pastures, and it's easy. All you have to do is turn more sharply than the bull. It doesn't take much to be brave if you have afición. There are lots of boys around who are as good or better who never get anywhere at all."

"I just know I can get you to that tienta!" Manolo

said earnestly. "You can cape the cows, and maybe even the bull they'll have for me. There will be all sorts of people there, and of course, the Count. When they see you, they're bound to know that you should be given a chance. They will help you."

"If only Castillo would be there!" Juan said dreamingly. "If only he would be there. He couldn't help me because he's no longer a critic, but I would so much like to meet him."

They had emerged into the ring again, and there was no more moon, the sky had clouded.

"Manolo, if you do get me to that tienta, I'll never forget it. But, I don't want you to kill yourself trying. You can ask if you wish, but I won't die if they won't let me come. I'm only fourteen. Sometime, somewhere, someone is going to see me and maybe get me a bull to fight. If not, I'll do what my father did before me. I'll get my chances at country fairs, at *capeas*. . . ."

"With bulls that have been fought before?"

"So what? I've already spilled my brave blood." He laughed.

"You mean, you have been gored?"

"Two years ago. About ten inches of horn in my right thigh. But I walk, and I can't even remember anymore if it was my fault or if the bull knew what he was doing."

They sat down in the stands. The moon came out again and the seats were silvery gray with its light.

"You see this plaza?" Juan asked, his eyes traveling around the ring. "This is my home. I want to live here. It's just that I'll have to wait. One day it will happen. I'll fight here—my own bulls. One day I'll fight not only here but in other bull rings. There may be others better than I, and maybe no one will pay too much attention to me, but I'll be good enough to give the crowd its money's worth. Because that's all I want to do, fight bulls honorably. The best way I can."

"But why do you? Why do you want so much to be a bullfighter?"

Juan laughed and stood up.

"It's not like wanting any other thing. It's in my blood, as it was in my father's. You're either born with it or, if you're not, somewhere, someplace you get infected. And there it is. You have afición, which just means that you'll never be happy doing anything else. But I am glad; don't think I'm not glad about it," he added proudly.

Manolo wished he could say that he did not feel that way at all. But he knew that it would be useless; he would not even be believed. If only Juan were his brother; then they would not expect him to be like his father, they would have someone else.

10

The day after he and Juan had broken into the bull ring, Manolo decided that he wouldn't try again to fight a bull. It would be just as they wanted: it would be at the ranch for the first time. But he could not forget how very good and how very brave Juan had been and how cowardly he himself had behaved. Nor did he forget his promise.

The next day he went to the café where the six men were always to be found, to talk to them about Juan.

"Manolo," one of them greeted him, "I am glad you did not go to the comic fight last night."

"'El Magnifico' was gored badly," another added.

It was not Juan's fault. Manolo was sure of that. Juan had not fought the bull long enough for that.

"When did it happen?" he asked.

"With the first pass."

"He tried a stupid trick, passing the bull on his knees much too close to the toril. The bull just rammed into him. He was blinded by the lights, confused by the noise. And the boy was too close, much too close, to the gate."

"We were about to go and see him. Come along with us."

On the way to the gored boy's house, Manolo listened to them tell about how bulls can hurt.

"The horn enters cleanly. If only it would exit that way. But either the man or the bull or both are moving at the time of the goring, and that's why the wounds are so bad."

"The horn tears into the body, ripping the muscles.'

"And there is always the danger of infections. The horn is dirty, and before penicillin, it was almost always either amputation or death from infection."

"As far as the bullfighters are concerned, penicillin was the greatest invention of man."

"Poor devils! When they get gored in small towns there is never a doctor."

"And that's where they usually get gored."

"Even here in Arcangel, there is only one doctor

who will touch a horn wound. Only one who knows anything about them, and he is getting old; when he is gone, maybe there will be no one."

"If you must get gored, be sure it's in Madrid."

"In Madrid they have a dozen doctors."

"I knew a doctor once who got rich on bullfighters. And then one day, he took his money and went to a printer and had millions of pamphlets printed. The pamphlet was called 'Stop the National Suicide'."

The men had never said anything before about pain, the amount of it a bullfighter had to endure. And Manolo had never thought before about pain. Now, listening to them, he thought that it would not be of dying that he would be afraid, but of the pain.

'El Magnifico,' lying on sheets that were as white as his face, looked to be about eighteen. The first thing Manolo noticed about him were his lips. They were pale, but he had been biting them. Drops of blood stood out in a row marking the places where the lips had been bitten. Without anyone having to tell him, Manolo knew that the boy was in great pain.

When they came into the room, 'El Magnifico' tried to hide his bloodied lips behind his hand. He did not say much, just that he was feeling all right. When he looked away from the men, he did not look out of the window, but at the wall where there was nothing but a stain. And when he turned back to them, his lips had fresh drops of blood on them.

"I was terrible," the boy said, trying to smile.

"You weren't there long enough," one of the men said "to let us see how terrible."

"I would have been very bad," 'El Magnifico' said, fighting back tears.

"You might have been fine. It was a good little bull. You were too brave, and sometimes it's silly to be too brave. You don't let the people see how long your courage is, just how wide."

The boy's mother came into the room. She was a big woman with strong hands and a face that seemed carved from a rock.

"The doctor's coming," she said not looking at the men but looking hard at her son. She waited for him to say something. He said nothing.

"Hasn't the doctor seen you?" one of the men asked.

The boy moaned and coughed to hide the sound of his pain.

"He was out of town," the mother said, looking now at them for the first time, her eyes accusing.

"The barber then, he took care of you in the infirmary?" the man wanted to know.

"Yes," the boy said, "he did the best he could."

"The barber's only a barber," the mother said angrily and left the room.

"He's in great pain. He doesn't show it, but he is in great pain," one of the men said softly to Manolo.

"It never hurts right after the goring. But when it starts hurting, it hurts for a long time," another added.

They heard footsteps outside. They were slow in reaching the door. The doctor was an old man. He shuffled when he moved from the door to the boy's bed. He looked tired. A shock of white hair fell listlessly over his wrinkled forehead as he bent over the boy.

"*Olá*. How goes it?" He smiled at the boy and passed his hand over the boy's forehead. He did not greet the men, nor did he seem to notice Manolo.

"The barber cleaned it and bound it," the boy said feebly, raising on his elbow and then falling back on the pillows.

The men began to move towards the door.

"Stay," the doctor said not looking at them, taking the light blanket off the boy's bed and reaching into his bag for a pair of scissors. "I want Olivar's son to see what a goring looks like. Come here," he commanded, and Manolo moved closer, his heart beating loudly. "Look!" The doctor had cut the bandage and the gauze and pushed them aside. A flamelike, jagged tear, a foot long and several inches deep ran straight from the boy's knee up his thigh. Manolo caught his breath at the sight of it. "Bend down and look here," the doctor said. "Those are puddles of clotted blood. There are about seven different reds beside, all meat. The muscles are purple. The wound is always narrower where the horn enters and wider where it exits. Not pretty, is it?"

Manolo moved away feeling sick; but the voice of

the doctor brought him back, and with its sound, so sure and matter-of-fact, the feeling of sickness left him.

"I'll need your help," the doctor said, still looking at but not touching the wound. "It's a good, clean tear. The barber did his work well. He took the dirt out and cut off the dead flesh."

When he walked to the washbasin, his feet were not shuffling. He scrubbed his hands thoroughly. He put the surgical towel on the bedside table, took some instruments from the bag, put them on the towel, and then reached for a package of gauze pads and put those next to the instruments.

"Hand me those gloves," the doctor said to Manolo, pointing to a pair of rubber gloves in a plastic bag. "Let's see how good a nurse you'd make," he added. "Open the bag without touching the gloves and hold them out to me." Manolo did as he was told.

Manolo watched fascinated, as the doctor's hands moved surely into the wound, exploring the inside of it.

"The horn stayed away from the thigh bone," the doctor said. "He's a lucky boy. What I am doing now," he explained, speaking to Manolo, "is looking for foreign matter; dirt, pieces of horn, or dead flesh. But as I said before, the barber did a very good job of taking all those out of the wound. There is no danger of infection."

The admiration Manolo felt for the doctor was

growing with each word, each gesture. No sound
came from the pillow. With tenderness the doctor
looked away from his work.

"He's fainted," he said with a smile. "Get the
bottle of ammonia," he motioned towards the bag,
"and a wad of cotton. Moisten the cotton and hold it
under his nose."

Again Manolo did as he was told. When he opened
the bottle, the strong odor of ammonia invaded his
nostrils and spread through the entire room. He bent
over the boy and passed the cotton directly under his
nose. The boy coughed and jerked his head away.

"Good!" the doctor said watching, "he's not in
shock. Just passed out from the pain. He will be fine.
What he's got is one of those lucky gorings." His
gloved hand pointed to the straight line of the torn
flesh, "It's as good a goring as you could wish for, if
you were wishing for a good goring. The bad ones
are the ones that tear in and change angles. Those are
the messy ones, the dangerous ones. But I don't want
you to think this is nothing. It's the result of foolishness. Not the beast's, but the man's. The beast is led
into the ring, the man walks in himself."

The doctor finished cleaning the wound and then
stitched the flesh. Manolo was not asked again to help.
He wished the doctor would once more request him
to do something. As he watched the magic way the
man's hands brought torn flesh together, he thought
that what the doctor was doing and had done was

the most noble thing a man could do. To bring health back to the sick, to cure the wounded, save the dying. This was what a man should do with his life; this, and not killing bulls.

"It will heal nicely. This one will. But then what?" The doctor walked to the wash basin and began washing the blood off the rubber gloves. "He," he pointed with his head to the boy, "will go on trying to prove that he can be good. And he isn't. But it's a point of honor with him. He will go on trying, and they will give him chances to try because he's fearless and the paying customers know that they will see a goring each time 'El Magnifico' is on the bill. But the tragedy is not that some people are bloodthirsty. The tragedy is that boys like him know of nothing else they want to do. I've grown old looking at wasted lives."

He walked over to Manolo and patted his head.

"The world is a big place," he said gently.

He seemed to want to add something, but he said nothing more. Silently, he put his instruments back in the bag and snapped it shut.

"Thank you for your help," the doctor said to Manolo, but his voice was tired now. The shuffle came back into his steps, and before he reached the door, he looked once again like a very old, very tired, man.

Walking back with the men, Manolo decided that if only he did not have to be a bullfighter he would be a doctor. He wanted to learn how to stop the pain and how to stop the fear of it. If only his father had been a doctor, a famous one, a bullfighters' doctor, then they would expect him to be one, too. And he would study hard. It would not be easy, but he would be learning to do something worthwhile.

He wondered if he were to tell the men, the six men, what he thought he would like to be, if they would listen to him. He looked at the men walking alongside him, talking once again about what they always talked about; and he knew that he would not tell them. He was who he was. A bullfighter's and not a doctor's son, and they expected him to be like his father.

He remembered suddenly his promise to Juan.

"There is," he said, interrupting their conversation about incompetent bullfighters, "one boy here in Arcangel who will be a great bullfighter if he is given a chance."

"Who's that, Manolo? Is it you?"

"No. His name is Juan García."

"We've never heard of him."

"Is he old García's boy?"

"The one who was a banderillero for your father for a while?"

"Yes."

"What about him?"

"I would . . . I mean, I promised to ask if he could come to the tienta."

"What for? You want him to fight your bull?"

"Oh no!" Manolo protested blushing. "But maybe . . . maybe the Count would let him make a few passes with . . . with a cow."

"Why are you asking this?"

"I promised I would."

"Is he a friend of yours?"

"Yes. And his brother is my very best friend."

"It means a lot to you?"

"I cannot break my promise."

"We'll write the Count."

"I'm sure he won't have anything against your inviting a friend."

"As long as he doesn't jump into the ring when you're fighting."

"Oh, he wouldn't do that! He'd never do that!"

"We'll write the Count today."

It was settled. He was sure that Juan would be allowed to come with him. He was also certain that the Count would let him make a few passes. And they would all be able to see how very good and how very brave Juan García was. Maybe then, seeing him, they would not care how terrible he himself was.

11

That night he lay awake thinking of the old doctor. After the tienta there would be no need to practice anymore; there would be time to do as he pleased after school and during the summer vacation. If the doctor would let him help around the clinic, he could learn much; even if it were nothing more than washing things and cleaning the place. The doctor was an old man and probably could use some help. After the tienta he would go to the doctor's clinic and ask.

But what if he got hurt with that first bull? That was more than possible. He must find a way of fooling the people. He must stand away from the bull's horns, so that they would not touch him. He would have his back to the people, and they would not see.

He got up and practiced the deception in front of the mirror. It seemed easy. But what of honor, he thought then. A most important thing, the *pundonor*. As a Spaniard, he could not live without it, or if he did, he would live in shame. It would be far better to be gored or even to be killed than to lose his sense of honor. No, he could not fool them because he could not fool himself. It would have to be done as was expected of him, with honor or not at all.

Manolo decided that he would pray instead to La Macarena, the patroness of bullfighters, pray to her to keep him safe. Each year the six men took him to Seville during the great fiesta that preceeded and followed Easter. They took him to see the official start of the bullfighting season. Next year in Seville, at that holy time, he would go alone to her shrine. He would sneak out of the hotel room one day and walk to La Macarena's shrine. He must promise her something in return. He did not know yet what it might be, but he would think of some sacrifice in exchange for her help. Her tear-stained face had always looked at him from his bedside. But in her own church she might hear his prayers better, he thought.

But Easter was far away, almost a year. And right after it would come the tienta. Manolo forgot neither. During that time, during all those months, he waited for both to come. Almost every night he practiced with the cape and the muleta and with his "sword." And on nights that he was tired and did not practice, he lay awake, praying sometimes, and sometimes with his eyes on the ceiling seeing shapes that would not be there in the morning.

He dreamed almost every night and was afraid to fall asleep because there were always bulls in his dreams now. Gigantic black animals with horns that never ended! They were always waiting for him. Not moving, just waiting. And there was always more than one bull. But, he, Manolo, was always alone. Alone in the bull ring with only the six men watching. They never said anything to him. He was alone inside the ring with the bulls, waiting, and he never did anything. He would just stand and wait, and the bulls would also stand and wait. Sometimes he would wake up screaming. Then his mother would rush in and comfort him. But he would never tell her about the bulls. He couldn't.

Many times during the day, and sometimes at night, he thought of the old doctor he had met at the house of "El Magnifico." He often walked past the doctor's house that also served as a clinic. He wished he could talk to the old man, could once again see him work. But he never went inside; it was not the right time. He envied those who did go in; they were not all sick or hurt. There were many who came bearing gifts: baskets with chickens, home-made bread, fruit, flowers, and wine. Each day, including Sundays, they came. Each to ask for the doctor's help or give him thanks. But Manolo could not ask for help or even advice on how one became a doctor, not now. Not when he had to do what he had to do.

Sometimes, too, he thought he saw the doctor looking at him, through the window or when they passed on the street. The doctor seemed almost about to say something, but he never did. Perhaps, Manolo thought, he, too, was waiting. If only he could get through the fight. But surely La Macarena would help him.

And finally, three weeks before the tienta, Holy Week arrived. But the men did not come for him. They did not come to take him to Seville. They left and said nothing. He would not even see La Macarena. Nothing could save him now. As the days went by, sometimes slowly, sometimes too fast, his fears multiplied and possessed his every waking moment and stayed with him during his recurring dreams. But there was no way out.

Then one day, at school during history class, a thought came to him that made him laugh aloud. What, what if his father had been afraid, too? Somewhere there might be an admission of it from his father, or from someone who knew him well, like Alfonso Castillo. There were a dozen books on the life of his father, besides Castillo's biography, and hundreds of articles bound into heavy volumes. If he looked among all these, he might find that his father too had been afraid.

He went that day, and the next, and the next, after school, to the museum's library. While looking, he learned more about bullfighting and more about his father's courage. He learned that the bravest of bulls and the bravest of bullfighters had always come from Andalusia. He learned about Belmonte and all the odds he had had to overcome to be the best, and about Joselito and how he, never having been gored, one day was killed by a bull. He learned about Manolete, and the way this "Knight of the Sorrowful Countenance" had lived and fought, and how in 1947, in Linares, he and a Miura bull killed each other. And he learned what it was that all great bullfighters had in common: willingness and courage. But he did not learn that his father had ever been afraid.

Yet the thought persisted. His father might also have been afraid. If not as a man, perhaps as a boy. He could not ask his mother, because she had always thought her husband a saint, and saints were not afraid. But he could ask his grandmother. She was the only one he would dare ask. After all, his father left from her house that day, at twelve, to fight his first bull. She might know; she would remember how it was with him at that age.

Manolo's grandmother was older than anyone he knew. Because she was so very old, she was almost deaf. She lived in a white house with flowerpots hanging from all the windows; and he used to visit her very often before he knew that he was expected to be like his father.

She opened the door for him, and he took her by the hand and led her to the middle of the room where no one from the street could hear them. He shouted loudly:

"Was my father ever afraid?"

"What are you saying?" She lowered her white head to his mouth.

"Was my father ever afraid?"

"Afraid of what?" she asked looking at him and straightening her back as far as it would go.

"Of bulls! Of being hurt, of being killed!"

"What?"

"Of bulls and dying and pain?" he shouted, now in tears.

"Your father was a great torero," she said proudly and trotted to the kitchen to get him a cookie. He did not wait.

12

When the six men came back from Seville, they avoided him. They let him pass on the streets as if he were a stranger or invisible. They had not forgotten him, he knew; they were remembering only too well that the time was almost at hand. Their teaching was over.

Three days before the testing of the bulls at the ranch of Count de la Casa, Manolo went to see Juan García. He could not stand being alone anymore with his fears and self-doubts. There was no turning back, but he must feel more sure that he would not disappoint those who believed in him. He thought that maybe Juan could tell from his cape work and from his passes with the muleta whether he was any good at all. But when he saw Juan he could not bring himself to ask. It was no use because it wasn't really the cape work that mattered. He needed to know if his knees would buckle under him in the ring, if there was enough strength in him to come out and cite the bull to charge. And the answer to that could not come from Juan.

What made it worse was the fact that Juan could hardly wait for the day.

"Do you think the Count will let me cape one of the cows?" he asked Manolo excitedly. "I know that he has invited Emilio Juarez and that he will be doing just that, caping the cows. But maybe, maybe they'll let me. You see," he continued with sincerity, "it's not because there will be people there who can help me, if I am good. I don't care about that at all. It's the animals. There will be at least ten cows to be tested. Ten cows that will have to be played with, to see how brave they are. Ten animals! Do you know what that means? Forty passes at least, with each. Four hundred! Four hundred times having an animal charge you! Do you know what I would give for a chance at all of them? I'd give my life."

How could it be, Manolo thought miserably, that this boy would happily die to do something he himself would rather die than do?

"For us," Juan continued, "it's tougher than for anyone else. A boxer can pick a fight, with anyone, anytime. But what good is training for us, if we can't train with an animal? And there are no animals. Do you know, Manolo, how many times I've had a bull charge me? Not more than fifty. Fifty stolen times: at night, with the seed bulls, too heavy, too angry. Most of those times it was no good at all. And then once, when I jumped into the ring in Seville. I got in three passes before they caught me. And then the night with you. You saw it. I was afraid of spoiling the animal for 'El Magnifico.' Do you know that at my age my father had already fought in ten capeas! Of course, the bulls had been fought before. But at least there were people watching. And you know, no matter what I say, you have to have an audience. It's important, very important. It's part of everything, the bull and what you do. You need people to yell, to cheer for you, or even against you. Manolo," he said, smiling, "you look as if you don't know how lucky you are. You look as if you don't know that you are the luckiest boy in Spain. And you know something else? You look as if you are doubting that you are going to be as good as your father."

"But I know that I won't!" He didn't mean to shout. "I mean," he said more quietly, not looking at Juan, "it seems no use. Being forced . . . made to do something I don't feel I am going to be any good at."

"You shouldn't feel that way. You should be saying to yourself that you'll be great. You know everyone, not only in Arcangel but in all Andalusia, in all of Spain, is waiting for the birth of a bullfighter. . . ."

"But why me?" The words tumbled out before he knew it. And suddenly he didn't want to hide anything from Juan anymore, except for his fears; he would still hide those. "Why not you?"

"Because your father . . ."

"Was Juan Olivar? But that doesn't make me anything but his son. Don't you see? Christopher Columbus had a son, but no one expected him to discover another New World!"

"Well, no, but . . ."

"It should be you, or someone like you, that they should be waiting for. Someone with talent, with afición, someone who wants very much to be a bullfighter."

"And you? You don't want to be a bullfighter?"

As Juan was asking the question, an idea came into Manolo's head, a wonderful, brilliant idea.

"Oh, Juan! I know what I should do. You will fight my bull!"

"What!"

"No, wait. It is only just; you and not I should fight. They will all be there, the rich people, the people who could help you. . . ."

"But . . ."

"Please! Your father never had a chance. If he had

had, maybe it would have been him and not my father who was the very best. And now you, you have everything; I saw you, you are very good! You have everything but a chance to prove that you are. And you can have that, don't you see."

"You're speaking very foolishly. This is your tienta and your bull."

"But who decided that? As long as they see a great bullfighter, they won't care what his name is."

"That's where you are wrong. It has to be an Olivar."

"Let me do it, Juan. I could talk to the Count. I could somehow convince him. It wouldn't mean anything to me, just to fight that bull; I swear to you, I'd rather, a million times rather, that you have your chance."

"I could never accept that sacrifice." Juan placed both hands on Manolo's shoulders. "That's one thing you cannot give me, Manolo. Your own chance at a life as a bullfighter. You might not yet know what it is to be looked up to. I want to be a hero, a very famous matador. I want everything that goes with it: the hard work and the money, the good and the bad bulls, the good and the bad days, the cars and the traje de luces, the applause and the booing. But this is not my time. This is your time to get started. My own time will come. I know it will. I am very sure of it. But this tienta is for you. For the son of Juan Olivar. And," he smiled again, his seriousness gone, "you will be my very best friend, for life. Because you offered to do something that only a very best friend could offer."

It is his pride, Manolo thought, that will not let him take my bull. And it was his own pride that would not let him insist. He felt sure that he could not please them, that he could never be what they expected of him. But he could not tell anyone.

That evening he walked by the Guadalquivir, alone. He could not study any more or think of anything else. It was not the fear any longer that bothered him, it was the lack of faith in his ability to even passably fight the animal. While walking along the banks of the black river, he thought of the things he had read about his father. His father, it seemed, had had a passion for bullfighting, he had wanted nothing more out of life than to face a bull. Could his father, Manolo wondered, ever have been made into something he was not? But, he argued with himself, his father had not even been interested in la fiesta brava before he faced that first bull. Why was it that he could fight so very well that first time and he, Manolo, feel so certain that he would not?

The cemetery gates were closed. Yet, by the light of the half moon he could see his father's statue. He stood looking at it for a long time trying to find the answer. And when he did, when he realized that it must have been the prophecy of the gypsy that made the difference, a cold shiver ran down his back.

13

The night before, he did not eat much dinner. Just enough for his mother not to worry about him. She did not say anything about the tienta. She sat quietly eating and not watching him. He liked that about her, he liked that very much, her not saying anything about tomorrow and her not watching him. And he liked the way she looked, proud and quiet. He knew, with nothing in particular to make him realize it, that he had a fine mother.

"Let's go for a walk," Manolo said to her after they finished dinner.

She went immediately to her room and came back wearing her black *mantilla*. Her hair, which was very black, looked even darker, and her face, which was always pale, even in the summertime, looked very white and very beautiful. Manolo was proud to walk with her. They walked to the river and then turned right, away from the cemetery.

"Tell me about my father," he said.

She did not say anything for a little while.

"He was a very tired man." She spoke with a deep Andalusian accent. "He never complained, but he was always tired those last two years. They asked too much of him, always more and more. Yet he never disappointed them. He gave more and more. Each time he was expected to be better than the time before. And not disappointing them made him tired. Sometimes, very often those last two years, I wondered how it was possible for him to go on. From one town to another, from one bullfight to the next, without enough sleep and without enough food.

"The summers were the worst. The heat wore him down more than the lack of sleep. You know, Manolo, I think your father was happy when he was dying, when he knew that he was going to die. I got there a few minutes before the end. He looked at me and recognized me. He never lost consciousness. He looked at me and said: 'It's good to rest.' And there was a smile on his face then and even when he died, he was still at peace; his eyes, the sad eyes that never smiled, looked as if they were finally, for the first time, smiling.

"He was always looking forward to the winters. The first year we were married, before you were born, we had the whole winter to ourselves. He was supposed to fight two benefit fights, but he had a bad cold and could not get up. I remember how sick he was, and how happy he was because he was sick. Not that he did not want to be a bullfighter. He always wanted that! He had it in his blood, all his life. But he liked to rest in the winter. By March he could hardly wait to fight again, but there were three, maybe four, months during the middle of the winter when he was happy because he did not have to fight.

"The second winter of our marriage things changed. He went to South America, to Mexico, to Colombia, Venezuela, and I don't know where else. That winter and all the other winters that followed, he traveled. He hardly ever had time to rest."

"Did he ever," Manolo asked, "want to give up being a torero?"

"Oh, yes," she answered, smiling, "each year. Each year after October, he threatened to give it up. But he never did. Others stopped for a year or two, or sometimes never went back. But he fought year after year for ten years. It seems strange! Your father was only twenty-two when he was killed. It seems strange because other young men only start their lives at that age."

The crescent of the moon was high in the sky reflecting in the dark waters. There was a soft breeze blowing, and the air was gentle with spring warmth.

"It will be a fine day tomorrow," his mother said quietly. "There will be hardly any wind. And there will be sun. Sun, and a clear sky, and no wind."

"How do you know?"

"I know," she said.

He knew himself how she was sure of it. She had been praying for such weather for him. Especially for no wind. And he was sure that she was right because he, too, had prayed for it.

"You know, Manolo." She put her hand on his shoulder. "It's a funny thing about the two of us. Both of us are always going to be haunted by your father. No matter what we do or what we say or what we are, we are part of him. And you know something else, it is not altogether a bad thing. It is rather a very fine thing. Mostly it's a fine thing because your father was a noble man. A man of honor. A man of pride. He would never do anything he did not really want to do. It is true, as I said, that the people expected him to be better and greater each time he faced a bull; but he, himself, also wanted that. And sometimes he was tired and had no time to rest; but he wanted it that way. The people, did not make him do anything he himself did not want to do. He willed it. Willed to be a torero, willed his life as it was, all the way to the end. That last bull, he knew that he should never have gone straight for the kill. He knew that the bull would hook into him. He knew that very well, no one had to tell him. But he wanted to kill the only way he found it honorable to kill, with no excuses. That was the great thing about your father: his own will to do what he was doing. What he did was for himself, most of all for himself."

They turned back and walked quietly towards the house. His mother's hand still rested on his shoulder. They were almost the same height, yet she seemed much smaller to him. Small and in need of protection in spite of her strength.

That night he could not fall asleep. They were coming for him at eight. He would not eat breakfast, not because anyone told him that he shouldn't, but because he knew a bullfighter fights on an empty stomach. He supposed it would be best to get as much sleep as possible and not to think. But he could not help thinking as he was lying in the dark. He thought about what his mother had told him, and he thought of what it would be like tomorrow. Finally he said one prayer after another, hoping that saying them would make him sleepy. And then, because that was a sinful thing to do, he got up and knelt in front of La Macarena.

"I wanted to come to your church. I wanted to offer you something. But it's too late now. Now I must ask you for a miracle and give you nothing in return. Let me be brave," he prayed looking at the beautiful face of the Mother of God. "And if . . . you could help me, just a little, that, too, of course. But let me not show fear. Let me not show that I am afraid. They have waited so long. They have been so patient and so good to me and to my mother. If I should be hurt, if after tomorrow I should be lame, they will see to it that I do not go begging in the streets. So I owe them as much for the future as I do for the past.

"I will not mind having only one arm or one leg. You must help me not to make them turn away from me in disgust. I must be brave because of them, and for my mother and not so much for my father. I think my father would not mind if I were a coward. He would not mind if I were not to go through with it because he would know that I want no part of being a bullfighter. If he were alive, he might even hide me from them. My mother cannot do that. But you, you can do anything. They think me a man, and you can make me one.

"And make the bull a little one to me, and very big to them; and make him not hate, but make him think that I am only playing with him. And if possible, please, don't let them make me kill the bull. If you could arrange it, dear Mother of God, so that I may be hurt before I have to kill the bull, please do that. Or make the bull so brave that they will leave him alone. So very brave that they will let him live.

"And if you can, please make me stand my ground.

That is part of my asking you for courage. No
matter what, don't make me run away from the bull.
Glue me to the sand. If you wish, make the bull kill
me, but don't let me disgrace my mother. Let me
die while she thinks me unafraid."

He slept a little towards morning and did not
remember, when his mother woke him, if he had had
any dreams, or even what day it was.

14

"It's a beautiful day." Juan García had been waiting in front of Manolo's house since six o'clock. "It's the most beautiful day I have ever seen in the fourteen years of my life. It is so beautiful that I want to cry. Do you feel the breeze? Manolo, there is just a whisper of a breeze! Not enough to move the muleta. It is the dream day of my life!" He threw up his arms and whirled around as a small child would do at Christmas time.

It was indeed a perfect day. A day for the bulls. With the sun, a man has a shadow, the bull has substance. And with no wind there is no danger of the lure blowing against the bullfighter's body.

"Manolo! I bless your mother and your father and I bless you for having done this for me. For taking me along." Juan had brought his own muleta, a shredded rug, stained with blood. "This was my father's," Juan said, unfurling it proudly. "He sold the cape when he needed money, and he even sold the sword; but he would never part with this."

When Manolo thought of what day it was, his throat became so dry he felt he would choke. Drinking water did no good at all. And listening to Juan he became aware of a tightness in the pit of his stomach and a great dryness that seemed to have spread through his body.

His mother brought out the box with his grandfather's cape and muleta. He watched her face to see if she could guess that he had taken them out. She did not seem to notice. She handed them to Manolo.

"I'm sorry they're not your father's," she said.

The men drove up at exactly eight o'clock. He wanted very much to kiss his mother, but he did not. Instead she passed her hand over his head, very briefly, and went inside the house without waving good-by.

"He looks fine," one of the men said. "He'll never show fear. He is like his father. Juan Olivar once told me that he was afraid all his life. Even before he was twelve. He was afraid like the rest of them, but the difference was that he never showed it. Not once."

Manolo listened in amazement. Why had they waited so long to tell him that? If he had only known this about his father! If he had only known that his father had also been afraid! Perhaps, after all, his own fears were groundless. Perhaps everything would turn out all right; he might even be able to fight as well as his father had that first time.

But it really did no good hoping or knowing. Nothing changed. Knowing that his father's fears had been as real as his own did nothing to dispel the choking dryness, the tight knot of fear in his stomach, nor the feeling that he had no afición.

"Every bullfighter is paralyzed by fear," another man said.

"Before and after, but not while fighting," Manolo heard Juan say. The men laughed.

" 'Not while fighting,' " he says, one of the men repeated, laughing. "Many are paralyzed much worse *during* than before or after."

"Not the good ones. Never the good ones," Juan said, and the men laughed again; not because what Juan had said was not true, but because the boy was so very serious and sure of himself.

"What do you know about all of this, about fear and bullfighters and all the rest?" they wanted to know.

"I know what I feel myself."

"But you don't look frightened?"

It was Juan who laughed now.

"But I am! Even though I am excited, more excited than ever before, I am also afraid."

"You don't sound like it," they insisted.

"Just try to make me spit," Juan said, smiling.

The men did not ask why he, Manolo, was so quiet. They left him alone. They talked among themselves of Emilio Juarez, the only professional bullfighter who would be at the tienta, and of the cows that would be tested. They did not mention Manolo's bull. But Juan asked them about it.

"What will Manolo's bull be like, do you know?"

"A three-year-old."

"Have you seen him?"

"Yes, we saw him."

"What does he look like?"

"A beautiful animal. A truly beautiful animal."

"What about the horns?"

"Comfortable. Quite comfortable. Not too open and not too closed. Big enough, but not too big. Just fine."

"Manolo! A fine pair of horns! Did you hear that?"

"He sounds very nice," Manolo said and was surprised at the sound of his own voice, calm and perfectly normal. He marveled at the miracle of having said what he had said in spite of the choking sensation in his throat.

"Will he be able to kill him?" Juan wanted to know.

"Of course!" one of the men said. "The Count

bred that animal especially for Manolo. And of course he will be able to kill him! Won't you, Manolo?"

"How would I know?" Manolo said, smiling at them.

"How does he know?" One of the men laughed. "How do you know who your father was?"

"I saw it in the newspapers," Manolo said, and they all laughed at the joke and patted him on the head.

The road was not paved and the old car bounced on it, its springs long gone. Manolo looked out of the window at the flat, rocky lands on one side and the olive groves on the other side. They were driving away from the mountains and into the low-hanging sun. It is a beautiful country, Manolo thought to himself, it is a beautiful land. He wondered if he would see it again. "If it is possible," he prayed, "don't let me lose my eyesight. Let it be a leg or an arm, but not my eyes."

"There will be eight cows tested today," he heard one of the men say.

"Will Manolo have his bull first, or will they test the cows first?" Juan asked.

"The Count said that Manolo would fight first."

So that was how it was going to be. Manolo listened quietly. It would be sooner than he had thought.

"The Count decided it will be best that way. Then Manolo, if he feels like it, can make some passes with the cows afterwards."

"Manolo's bull, will it be picked?" Juan wanted to know.

"There will be no picador," one of the men answered. "The animal is only a three-year-old. If one fights a young bull intelligently, it is ready for the kill, and the kill is not a problem."

"Juan Olivar's bull was supposed to be picked, but he didn't want it. He dismissed the picador. Manolo will be able to do the same, fight the animal brilliantly and kill him without the help of a picador."

"The bull will spill blood only once. As it should be."

"It will be the last part, the faena that will be most important. Fought well with the muleta, any bull, even a six-year-old, can be ready for the kill, with its head down, when the torero is ready."

"Manolo will be able to do all this. Able to fight intelligently with both the cape and the muleta. He does not want to have it any other way."

No, Manolo realized suddenly, he did not want to have it any other way. It must be just like his father. If he had to do it, he must do it just like his father. And at that moment he became certain that La Macarena would answer his prayers. She would make him brave. And perhaps because she would make him brave, he would have to die. But he would do it as his father had done it.

"You probably can't wait," one of the men was saying to Juan, "to know if the Count will let you make a pass or two."

"Do you think he will? Do you?"

"You must think that," the man said, "since you came with your muleta. And since you've already told us of your fear."

"Oh, I just brought it along, in case."

"Don't you use a cape?" another asked.

"I don't have one."

"Have you ever tried it with a cape?"

"Oh yes! I can make veronicas but nothing else. Just veronicas and medias."

"Like Juan Olivar!"

"It's just because I haven't had many chances with the cape."

"Where do you practice?"

"With the bulls."

They didn't believe him and laughed.

"Not many times," Juan said. "But almost always with the bulls. Just once I practiced a couple of passes without a bull."

"Where do you fight your bulls?"

Juan hesitated.

"On the pastures," he said finally. "But always with the seed bulls. I wouldn't take any other."

They laughed again.

"I swear it's the truth. Just once I made a few passes with a bull that was going to be fought. And just once I jumped in on someone else's bull."

"Well! We must see today what you can do."

"But you must not try Manolo's bull. Manolo will fight him alone. It's going to be all his. Not even

Emilio Juarez is going to touch Manolo's bull."

They said that very firmly. Protectively and proudly. Manolo heard them. It was to be his bull. No one else's. What had they said about the horns? Big, but not too big, comfortable. How very close would they be comfortable? He would be close as possible, so very close that people would gasp. It would be hard to make the six men gasp. It would be hard to please them. But he was sure now that he would be good enough to make them happy. And if he was, if he did make them proud and happy, and if by some miracle, he lived, would he have to do it all over again? How soon? The thought was a new one; he had never thought beyond the first fight. But now, he wondered why he had never understood. This was not the end. What had Juan said? All Spain was looking for the birth of a bullfighter. That did not mean one fight.

He could see the gate to the ranch now, and beyond it the round circle of the bull ring.

15

He had not realized that there would be quite so many people. They filled the high-ceilinged living room, but did not dwarf its height. They stood in groups, and some were seated on massive chairs and couches. All of them, and there were almost a hundred, wore hunting clothes; Manolo wondered grimly if they had just come from a hunt or if they were just going to one.

He looked around the great room's walls, at the photographs of the Count's best breeds and at the five mounted bulls' heads next to and above the gigantic fireplace. He wished he could stand in this great room alone. Alone, it would seem a pleasant place.

The Count came towards him, one thin, bony hand extended in greeting.

"Manolo! We've all been waiting."

He saw only a blur of smiling faces as the Count raised his voice to introduce Juan Olivar's son. It seemed to Manolo that no dream he had ever had was more unreal. He felt nothing, neither his legs, carrying him from person to person, nor his fingers, being grasped by strangers' hands. His mind was numb and so was his tongue. The tight knot that had once been his stomach and the choking that had been his throat seemed to have been present always; it was as if he had been born and had always lived with these twin sensations.

The Count introduced him last to a gaunt gentleman seated in a wheelchair.

"This is Alfonso Castillo."

There had been no photographs taken of the famous bullfight critic. Manolo had often imagined what he looked like. He had thought the man a giant, something more than a man and a little less than a god. Only Castillo's deep eyes measured up to this vision. His body, under a blanket cover, must have been broken, yet Manolo had never heard that Castillo was a cripple. They did not shake hands; Castillo's hands remained poised on his knees.

"It's ridiculous that you should be here," he said

unsmiling, his strange eyes hard. "I thought that at the last minute the town of Arcangel would refrain from trying to repeat history in this nonsensical fashion. But you are here, where only the ghost of your father rightfully belongs."

"Why shouldn't the boy be here?" Emilio Juarez approached them and put his hand on Manolo's shoulder. "Tientas are not for ghosts but for boys like Manolo, boys who have waited a long time to prove how brave they are."

"Has anyone," Alfonso Castillo asked of no one in particular, his bottomless eyes still fixed on Manolo, "has anyone asked the boy if it is his wish to be here? It seems to me that we have taken upon ourselves God's prerogative: playing with the destiny of a human being. Even God does not tamper with free will."

Emilio Juarez smiled and, bending towards Manolo's ear, whispered: "How do you feel? Happy, and also a little scared, I hope."

"Alfonso!" the Count protested. "Need you ask if the boy wishes to be here? Just look at him. He, like everyone else, has been waiting for this day." The Count put his arm around Manolo. "Come with me to the study, I want to show you something. Come along with us, Alfonso."

"I would not like to miss this," Castillo said sourly, and, declining the Count's offer to wheel the chair, steered himself toward two carved doors. The Count and Manolo followed.

The Count was pushing apart the great doors as Juan García approached the wheelchair.

"Señor Castillo," the boy began timidly.

"What is it?" Castillo asked impatiently.

"I . . . I would very much like . . . to shake the hand of the greatest of critics."

"Who are you?"

The Count turned to Manolo and also asked who the boy was.

"He's my friend, Juan García." With this, Manolo spoke for the first time since entering the Count's house. "You gave me permission to bring him."

"You have not heard of me," Juan was saying to Castillo and blushing a violent red.

"But, undoubtedly, I will." Castillo smiled and the smile lit up his gaunt face. He no longer looked forbidding or mysterious. "You'll be a great torero someday?"

"If it is the will of God."

Alfonso Castillo extended his hand:

"I wish you God's will then."

"Come on in," the Count said to Manolo as Alfonso Castillo steered his chair inside. "I'll close the doors."

With the doors closed, the room was quite dark. The Count walked to the window and pulled on a drape cord. As the drapes drew apart, a shaft of light illuminated the fireplace and above it, a painting. Manolo gasped with surprise. The painting was of a boy who looked exactly like himself.

"This is your father," the Count said, "at this ranch with his first bull. The painter painted it from his memory, an excellent one."

"Don't admire the closeness of your father's body to the bull," Castillo said, moving his chair closer to the painting, "nor the gentleness with which he seems to be guiding the animal with the muleta. I want you to look at your father's face. What do you see in his face?"

Manolo looked up at the face of the boy; it was not quite like his own face, he saw. There was something more than just seriousness on it, more than concentration, and more than sadness.

"It is," he said slowly, "the face of a boy . . . becoming a man."

"Exactly, and well said!" Castillo's voice seemed proud of Manolo's answer. "At that precise moment your father was leaving his childhood behind. And he was happy to be doing it at twelve. He was not only becoming a bullfighter, he was also taking on the responsibility of being a man."

The Count pointed to the wall opposite.

"This is the head of the bull your father killed that day."

A giant head of a black bull looked down at Manolo. Its horns were long and sharp; its eyes, open, stared glassily. It was much too big, the boy thought; it was as big as "Patatero's" head. But the eyes of the bull were different, not as frightening as those of his father's killer.

"His name was 'Castalon'," the Count said. "Your bull today is called 'Castalon the Second'. It is as fine an animal as this one. I would say that it deserves the same fate as this one. A great faena from a great torero."

Manolo, his eyes on the floor, knew that the Count was waiting for a reply, waiting for assurance that he, Manolo, would try his best. But the words would not come.

"Would you leave us alone for a moment?" It was Castillo who had spoken. Manolo did not look up to see the Count leave. But he did look at Alfonso Castillo when he began to speak.

"The fate of a brave animal should never be anything but a noble death after a noble fight. But it is not the same with a man's fate. A man is not like a fighting bull. A man's life should not be all fighting, but also giving, loving. A man's life is many things. Before he becomes a man, he has many choices: to do the right thing, or to do the wrong thing; to please himself, or to please others; to be true to his own self, or untrue to it."

For the first time since he had awakened that morning, Manolo felt the reality of hearing words and seeing things. It was not that the fear had left him, it was still inside of him, but his mind was functioning. He repeated to himself Castillo's last words. His mother had said almost the same thing to him when she spoke of his father.

"No one but your father really knew why it is that I am sitting here, in this chair, rather than standing next to you." Alfonso Castillo's voice was no longer gruff, but soft. "Some ten years ago, a bullfighter who claimed I ruined his career by my criticism of it, challenged me to fight a bull. I could have laughed him off. At first I did; and then I wondered if I had rejected the challenge out of intelligence or out of cowardice. I was on my way to a ranch where I was going to find out the answer when my car ran off the road. I think it was the fear I felt while driving toward the bull that caused the accident. Just thinking about coming face to face with the animal, I discovered how powerful fear can be. While writing about bullfighters, I was aware that they feared the danger of gorings, of death, but I thought them to be brave men because they were able to conquer the fear, able to drive it far away from their minds, to be free enough of it to do their jobs. That day, because of the accident, I did not find out if I could do that. But since that day I've encountered other fears, in all kinds of situations. And since that time I have found that you cannot confuse bravery or courage with lack of fear. Real courage, true bravery is doing things in spite of fear, knowing fear."

Alfonso Castillo had been looking at the portrait of Juan Olivar as he talked. Now he faced Manolo.

"But I did not mean to talk about myself. I wanted to give you advice. Adults are always doing that; it's one of their occupational hazards. Don't let people push you. If you are honest with yourself, you will do the pushing. But only when it is important, important to you. I knew your father well, maybe better than any other person he ever considered his friend. If he were alive, I am sure you would not be here today. He would have understood that you are not a carbon copy of him, and you would have known it also. I do not think you want to be a bullfighter. I do not believe you are like your father. Be what you are, and if you don't yet know what you are, wait until you do. Don't let anyone make that decision for you."

"The boy you met, Juan García, there is nothing he would not do to be a bullfighter."

"I read that in his face."

Castillo waited for Manolo to say something else, but there was no need now. Suddenly it seemed that the burden he had carried for so long, weighing him down, was gone. And he also knew that the people who had come to see him, wearing their hunting clothes, were going to attend a hunt. But the quarry would not be caught by them but by him, Manolo Olivar.

"Thank you," Manolo said gratefully, "thank you, Señor Castillo, for helping me to make a decision."

"Whatever it is, I feel it is the right one," Alfonso

Castillo said, shaking Manolo's hand. "Remember, Manolo," he added, "in the end it is all between you and God."

Before leaving the room, Manolo looked up at the face of his father and felt that maybe today he, too, was going to become a man.

They walked across the cobblestone courtyard toward the circular enclosure of the bull ring. A gentle breeze moved the leaves on the old maples that surrounded the courtyard and lined the road leading into town. It was strange, Manolo thought, how much brighter the sky looked, how much warmer the sun felt on his back. The fear, though still there as before, was no longer paralyzing.

Emilio Juarez and Manolo walked side by side across the sand, and together they slid behind the *burladero*.

"It's a sweet animal," Emilio Juarez said.

Manolo looked at the triple tier of balconies filling up with the people in their hunting clothes. The Count and Alfonso Castillo were seated in the first row, in the center. Juan, also in the first row, was flanked by the six men, their faces tense with the anxiety of waiting. To one side, and removed from the others by a few empty seats, sat the old doctor. His face, unlike the faces of the others, looked tired.

There was no bugle, just the clanking of the chain, and Manolo saw a gate open and the gaping blackness beyond. He slid out, the cape firm in his hand, his legs, not numb anymore, carrying him to the center of the ring.

"*Ehe, toro!*"

The animal seemed to shoot out of the darkness, its black skin shining in the sun, its hoofs thundering louder by far than the beating of Manolo's heart. He did a veronica, and he knew he had done it right even before the *olé* rang out. He had been very close, and the cape had moved slowly and smoothly just in front of the bull's head. Does it have horns? he thought in the instant that it took the bull to turn and recharge. On the second time he saw them, saw them, long and smooth and gray, almost touch the magenta of the cape, and he did not know whether the people had screamed their approval or not. But on the third veronica, he heard them again; and this time his hands seemed suspended, together with the profile of the bull's head, right below his eyes, right next to his body. Three times more, each time feeling the beauty of what he was doing, Manolo let the bull brush against him, heard the bull's breath expelled through its wide nostrils, its hoofs moving the earth under them both. And then, with the gentleness of a caress he let the cape balloon and fall behind him in a media-veronica that brought the animal to a standstill behind his back.

They were on their feet, applauding and shouting as he looked towards them. Their faces seemed blurred, and he did not know if there were tears in his eyes. He moved away from the resting bull, deciding that he would do the fancy passes, the ones he knew he could do. He did five chicuelinas and then six reboleras, and they shouted their joy. Now he himself was shouting, too, loving the ease with which his body obeyed him, loving the animal for following so perfectly the lure of the moving cape. And when he was through, the bull nailed to the sand with another close, perfect media-veronica, he walked proudly to the burladero to get his muleta, the shouts and the clapping making his back very straight, his head very high.

"Wonderful," Emilio Juarez said. "You were wonderful."

He handed Manolo a wooden sword and the muleta. Manolo's hands trembled as he slid the sword underneath the red cloth. He didn't like that, and he hoped that Emilio had not noticed.

"Give them a great faena," Emilio said patting him on the back.

I'll do a series of naturales and derechasos, Manolo thought, just those, nothing more, and I'll do them well. But his knees were no longer strong; they seemed to buckle under him as he ran out. He was remembering the problems he had had with the muleta. The passes were so difficult. He had never been pleased with them. Never in all those nights. This then would be the time when he would know.

And it would be as he had decided, when he was in there with Castillo. If he did well, he would be a bullfighter; not because they wanted it but because he wanted it. But if he knew, knew as he fought the bull, that this was not what he wanted, then he would tell them so. He would not be pushed into what he did not want. No one could say that he had not tried. And he, himself, would know that he was brave.

"*Ehe toro!*" He meant to shout it, but it came out as a whisper. "*Ehe toro!*" He repeated it again louder, but not the same as the first joyful cry, the cry with the cape.

As the bull moved, Manolo tried to change his hands; it would be better not to try it with his left, but to do it with his right. He needed more distance, he thought; but the animal was almost upon him. He jumped back without having made a pass and was surprised to see that the muleta was no longer in his hand but on the bull's tossing head. Emilio Juarez ran out, lifted the cloth off the horns, and shouted to Manolo.

It is no use, Manolo thought, concentrating all his will power on making his tired legs move toward Emilio. From now on it would be cheating them. He could see that. He had proved to himself that he could do it, but he was not good enough for the faena; and he did not want to be. When the bull rushed toward him, he kept his ground but the pass, a derechaso, was made jerkily, far too short. The bull recharged very fast, and Manolo was not yet ready for him. All he managed this time was an inept movement of the hand that brought the bull's neck in a punishing twist toward the ground.

It was time to make a decision. Either he went on cheating them, and himself, or he did the thing he knew now he must do. He was right below the seats. He looked up at the Count and then at Castillo, and it was to Castillo that he spoke:

"I will not fight this brave bull." The voice, strong and loud, sounded unfamiliar to Manolo. "I am not like my father. I do not want to become a bullfighter."

"But, Manolo!" It was the Count. "You were magnificent with the cape. Perhaps you need a little work with the muleta, but that can be done. Go on, boy. You will be very good."

"No." Manolo was very sure now. "If I were to become a bullfighter, I would be like 'El Magnifico'; but at least he has afición. I do not. It is because I do not want to cheat you that I will not continue. You came to see a bullfighter born. There is a boy here who could be as great as my father was. His name is also Juan."

He did not ask the Count's permission but walked a few steps toward Juan.

"This is your bull, Juan."

"But, Manolo . . ." the Count protested. Then looking at Castillo and again at Manolo, he said stiffly, "All right, let the boy fight."

As he jumped into the ring, tears ran down Juan's cheeks. His face looked quite blurred to Manolo, because he, too, had tears in his eyes.

As he turned, he looked up at the six men, expecting to see anger and disappointment written plainly on their faces. But if it had been there, it was gone. For Juan was in the ring and the men were watching breathlessly as he took the bull in a brilliant series of naturales. They, and everyone else, were on their feet. Shouts of *Olé* echoed through the enclosure.

Manolo walked slowly to the empty seats. The old doctor motioned for him to sit down.

"Now," said the doctor gruffly, "you will have time to come to my clinic after school. I need help there."

"I'd like that."

"You didn't fool me," the doctor said. And for the first time a smile lit up his wrinkled face. "I knew you were no bullfighter. But I did think, after seeing you just that once, that you might make a fine doctor. You think that, too, don't you? And you know that I intend to help you."

"Yes, sir," For the first time, in what seemed like a long time, Manolo smiled, too.

"Don't think you'll become a doctor without cleaning floors and washing bedpans. That's what you'll be doing, at first. The learning will take time. And hard work."

"I know."

Then in silence he and the doctor watched Juan García, fourteen, and the bull "Castalon the Second," make bullfighting history. As he watched them, there was a sadness in Manolo, but no jealousy. Sadness, for there was much beauty in the sight on the yellow sand and he was not part of that beauty. But there was no jealousy because he was sure what it was he wanted to do with his life. And his father's life, bullfighting, would stay a part of him, as it always had been, but in a different way than anyone had planned.

Glossary of Bullfighting Terms

Afición (*ah-fee-see-own*), love for bullfighting; also refers to a group of people who are familiar with bullfighting; bullfight fans.

Aficionado (*ah-fee-see-own-ah-doh*), dedicated fan of the art of bullfighting, also amateur bullfighter.

Alguacil (*ahl-wah-ceel*), mounted constable who opens the bullfight by riding ahead of the bullfighters and who relays the orders of the president of the bull ring to the bullfighters. He is always dressed in a Philip II costume.

Alternativa (*ahl-ter-nah-tee-vah*), ceremony in which a *novillero* becomes a *matador de toros*.

Banderillas (*bahn-dah-reel-yahs*), steel-barbed wooden shafts, about 28 inches long, decorated with paper. These are placed in the bull's withers after the *picadors* have retired and before the bullfighter begins working with the *muleta*. *Banderillas* are placed in pairs, six in all, either by the bullfighter himself or one of his *banderilleros*.

Banderillero (*bahn-dah-reel-yero*), one whose duty it is to place *banderillas*. Each bullfighter, during a formal *corrida*, has three *banderilleros* who also assist the bullfighter in testing out the bull's charges.

Barrera (*bah-re-rah*), wooden fence around the arena; also first row of stands or seats running around the bull ring.

Burladero (*boor-lah-they-roh*), narrow opening into the arena with wooden shield in front. This acts as protection for the men who can enter and leave from the sides. It stands about a foot away from the fence and several of these are found long the circular fence that encloses the bull ring.

Callejón (*cahl-eh-hone*), passageway between the *barrera* and the stands. This is where the bullfighter's *cuadrilla*, if not inside the ring or behind the *burladero*, is found. Some members of the press, especially the photographers, are usually allowed inside the passageway which is otherwise reserved only for bullfighters, their helpers and the bull breeder.

Capea (*cah-pay-ah*), informal bullfight in small villages where there are no bull rings in which amateurs and aspirant bullfighters take part without the benefit of *picadors*. These events are usually held during local *fiestas* and the bulls used have more often than not been fought at other *capeas*.

Chicuelina (*cheek-well-ee-nah*), cape pass invented by the bullfighter Chicuelo in which the bull passes by the man's side and not in front of him.

The man offers the cape to the bull and as the bull charges, the man makes a pirouette in which the cape wraps itself around his body. At the end of the turn the man faces the bull to make another *chicuelina*.

Corrida de toros (*cor-ree-da deh tor-rohs*), or simply *corrida*, literally a running of the bulls; a bullfight. One may say, I am going to *una corrida*; or *a los toros*.

Cuadrilla (*cwa-dreel-yah*), the *matador's* helpers, his *banderilleros*, *picadors* and sword handler (*mozo de estoque*).

Derechaso (*deh-re-chah-soh*), see *natural*.

Faena (*fah-eh-nah*), the last and the most important part of a bullfight when the *muleta* is used.

Fiesta (*fee-yes-tah*), feast day, holiday, a saint's name day.

Fiesta Brava (*fee-yes-tah*, *brah-vah*), literally, the brave spectacle; a bullfight.

Fiesta de los Toros (*fee-yes-tah-day loss tor-rohs*), literally, the feast of the bulls; a bullfight.

Ganadería (*gahn-nah-deh-ree-ah*), ranch where the fighting bulls are raised. Also the particular strain of brave bulls.

Ganadero (*gahn-nah-deh-roh*), a breeder of brave bulls.

Gaonera (*gah-oh-neh-rah*), a cape pass named after its inventor, the Mexican bullfighter, Gaona. It is done during the *quite* by holding the cape behind the man's body and luring the bull past the man's chest.

Lidia (*lee-dee-ah*), combat; bullfight; also used in "toros de lidia" meaning fighting bulls.

Mandar (*mahn-dahr*), literally, to send on; to control. It means to excert mastery over the bull and not let the animal dominate but rather make it obey the cloth, either the cape or the *muleta*.

Mantilla (*mahn-tee-ah*), lace head covering used in Spain by the women. While women wear almost always a black *mantilla*, young girls often wear white. In Andalusia during *fiestas* the women wear *mantillas* over large combs and the lace falls over their hair like veils.

Manzanilla (man-zah-nee-yea), light, dry sherry wine, drunk in Andalusia by everyone associated with bullfighting.

Mariposa (*mah-ree-poh-zah*), literally, butterfly, a pass with the cape held over the shoulders, the man facing the bull. The man zig-zags slowly backwards luring the bull with one, then the other side of the cape. Invented by Marcial Lalanda, it is used during the *quites*.

Matador (*mah-tah-dohr*), killer; killer of bulls; a bullfighter who has received his *alternativa*.

Media Veronica (*meh-d-ya veh-roh-nee-kah*), half-*veronica*. After a series of *veronicas* the man gathers the cape to one side of his body and the bull is made to take a very sharp turn following the cape and has to pause from the exertion of turning his neck at a sharp angle.

Monosabios (*moh-noh-sah-bee-yos*), literally, wise monkeys; the ring attendants whose chief function is to help the *picadors* to maneuver into position.

Montera (*mohn-teh-rah*), the black hat worn by bullfighters.

Muleta (*moo-leh-tah*), red flannel cape used in the last part of the bullfight. It is heart-shaped and draped over a wooden stick. The *muleta* may be held in the right hand, over the sword, and passes made thus are called *derechasos*. Or it may be held in the left hand; these are the most dangerous of passes, since the distance between bull and bullfighter is considerably reduced; these left-handed passes are called *naturales*.

Natural (*nah-too-rahl*), see above. The classic pass with the *muleta* in which the bull follows the palm of the bullfighter's hand. Fundamental pass of bullfighting, the most emotional of all and most dangerous when done with the left hand. (Some people call passes done with the right hand *natural con la derecha* but *derechasos* is the more commonly used name.)

Novillada (*noh-veel-yah-dah*), bullfight with bulls under four years of age.

Novillero (*noh-veel-yeh-roh*), a bullfighter before he takes his *alternativa;* one who fights *novillos*.

Novillo (*noh-veel-oh*), a bull under four years of age.

Número Uno (*noo-meh-roh oo-noh*), literally, number one, or the best; the champion.

Olé (*oh-lay*), roughly "bravo"; shout of approval heard at bullfights and also during performance of flamenco dancing and singing.

Parar (*pah-rahr*), literally, to stand one's ground; to keep the feet from moving away from the bull's charge.

Pase de pecho (*pah-seh deh pe-choh*), chest pass made with the *muleta* held in the left hand at the finish of a series of *naturales*. The bull charges by the man's chest and is sent away with a forward sweep of the *muleta*.

Paso-doble (*pah-soh doh-bleh*), music played at bullfights. When played during the *faena* it is as homage to a great fight. Many *paso-dobles* were written in honor or memory of great bullfighters. Also a two-step music which can be danced to.

Picador (*pee-cah-dorr*), a mounted man whose mission it is to slow down the bull's charges and abate his energy by wounding him in the withers with the *pura*, a pick to which an iron shaft is attached. Strict rules govern the picking of the bulls, but unfortunately they are not always observed in spite of the fact that over-picking is punishable by fines and the ire of the crowd.

Plaza (*plah-zah*), usually the main square of the town; *plaza de toros* means bull ring.

Pundonor (*poon-doh-norr*), honor, a most precious quality to a Spaniard, a sense of obligation to do one's best at all times which honorable bullfighters feel and dishonorable ones lack.

Querencia (*kway-rain-see-ah*), bull's arbitrary refuge inside the arena; literally, beloved spot. Bulls which are not particularly brave always chose a spot inside the bull ring to which they return or sometimes do not want to leave at all. Their charges, when lured away from the *querencia*, can be extremely dangerous because they are on the defensive; but as they head back to their *querencia*, they are not at all dangerous and the bullfighter is said to have a "free tip" on such a pass. Not only cowardly bulls search out and find their "beloved spot," brave bulls also do this; such spots are often in the place where the horse has stood or the bull's blood had been spilled.

Quite (*kee-tay*), the act of taking the bull away from the horse or from a man who is in danger or has been gored. The passes used in taking the bull away from the *picador* are the fancy passes such as *mariposas, gaoneras, chicuelinas*. When a *quite* is made to save a bullfighter, it is merely a movement of the cape to distract the bull's attention.

Rebolera (*ray-boh-lay-rah*), a cape pass which ends a series of *quites* or *veronicas* in which the man swirls the cape in a circle around himself as he stands still and brings the bull to a sharp stop.

Templar (*tem-plah-rr*), to adopt the movement of the lure to the speed of the charging bull. It is the aim of the bullfighter to make the passes as slowly as the bull will allow without hooking into the lure. It is, of course, up to the bullfighter to try to impose the desired speed on the animal. Unfortunately those who are not able to *mandar* and *parar* can never hope to be able to *templar*.

Tienta (*tee-yen-tah*), testing of the young bulls and heifers. The bulls are tested only with *picadors* to determine their bravery in receiving punishment. The pic used is much smaller than that used during bullfights. The cows are tested both on foot and by *picadors*. The *ganadero* observes these testings most carefully to determine how the animals will be mated, and whether or not the bulls are to be sent to bullfights as *novillos* or full-grown.

Toreo (*toh-ray-oh*), the art of bullfighting.

Toreristas (*tohr-ray-ree-stahs*), fans of the bullfighters as opposed to those who give their preference to the bulls and admire the animals more than they do the men who fight them.

Torero (*tohr-ray-roh*), bullfighter; this term also includes *banderilleros*, *picadors* and *matadors* as *novilleros*. But to say: "he is a great *torero*" is to refer only to the *matador*.

Toril (*tohr-reel*), the gate through which the bull comes into the arena; commonly known as the gate of fears.

Toristas (*tohr-ree-stahs*), those who admire the bulls and know more about them than they care to know about the *toreros*.

Toro de bandera (*tohr-roh deh bahn-deh-rah*), a bull superior in bravery.

Traje de luces (*trah-hee deh loo-cez*), suit of lights, formal bullfighter's dress worn at all professional bullfights except benefit fights and *capeas*.

Veronica (*vay-roh-nee-kah*), the most classic of all cape passes, one which proves or disproves, depending on how it is done, the bullfighter's real art with the cape. It is done by holding the cape with both hands and moving it smoothly in front of the bull and alongside the man's body. Because when the cape is offered to the bull it looks like the handkerchief St. Veronica offered to Christ, it has been named in honor of that saint.